# MORE EASY PIANO TUNES



**Anya Suschitzky**

**Edited by Anthony Marks**

**Designed and illustrated by Simone Abel**

**Original music by Anthony Marks and Anya Suschitzky**

**Arrangements by Anya Suschitzky**



**Music engraving by Poco Ltd, Letchworth, Herts**

First published in 1993 by Usborne Publishing Ltd, Usborne House, 83-85 Saffron Hill, London EC1N 8RT, England.
 Printed in Portugal.

This book has lots of tunes for you to play on the piano. They can also be played on the electronic keyboard. As you go through the book the tunes get more difficult and may need more practice. At the end there are some tunes for two people to play.

Throughout the book there are lots of hints on how to improve your playing. There are also facts about different kinds of keyboard instruments and the composers who wrote music for them.

The section called "Music help" on page 62 explains the Italian words, music directions and key signatures used in the book. It also contains hints on practice and suggestions of music to listen to.

## Carefree

### Sharps and flats

The sharps and flats at the beginning of a tune are called the key signature. They tell you which notes to play sharp or flat throughout the tune.

A sharp raises a note by a half step or semitone (see page 50).

A flat lowers a note by a half step or semitone.

### Accidentals

Sharps, flats and naturals that are not in the key signature are called accidentals. They are added to the staff in front of the note they change.

An accidental only applies to the notes in the bar in which it appears. In the next bar you go back to the original key signature.

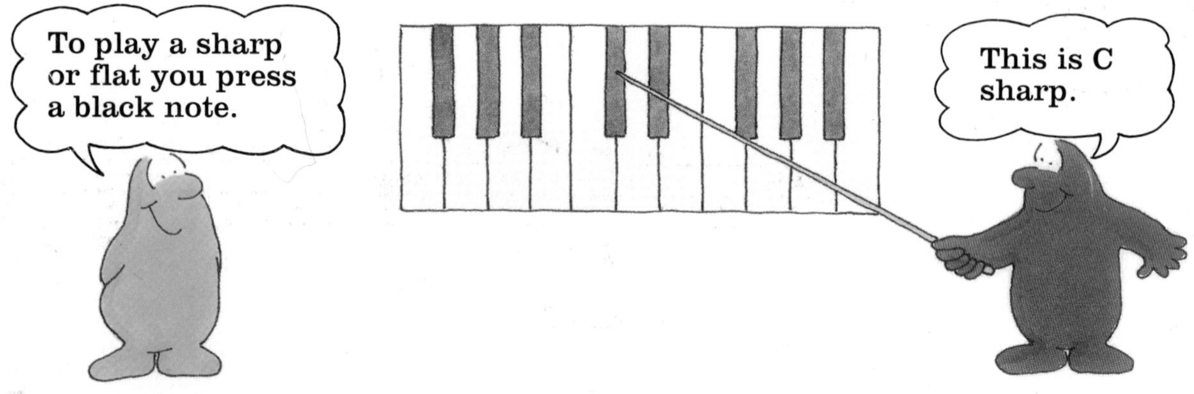

# When the saints

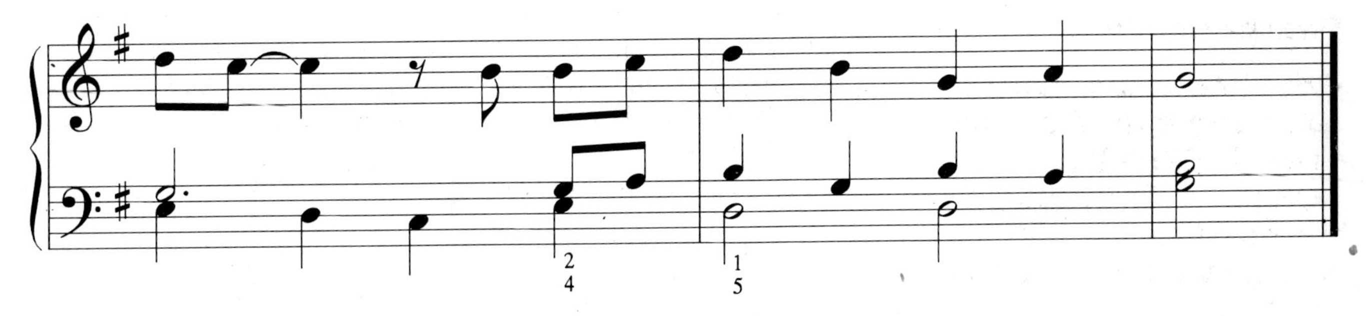

## Ledger lines

To find out which note to play, count up or down from the last note on the staff like this.

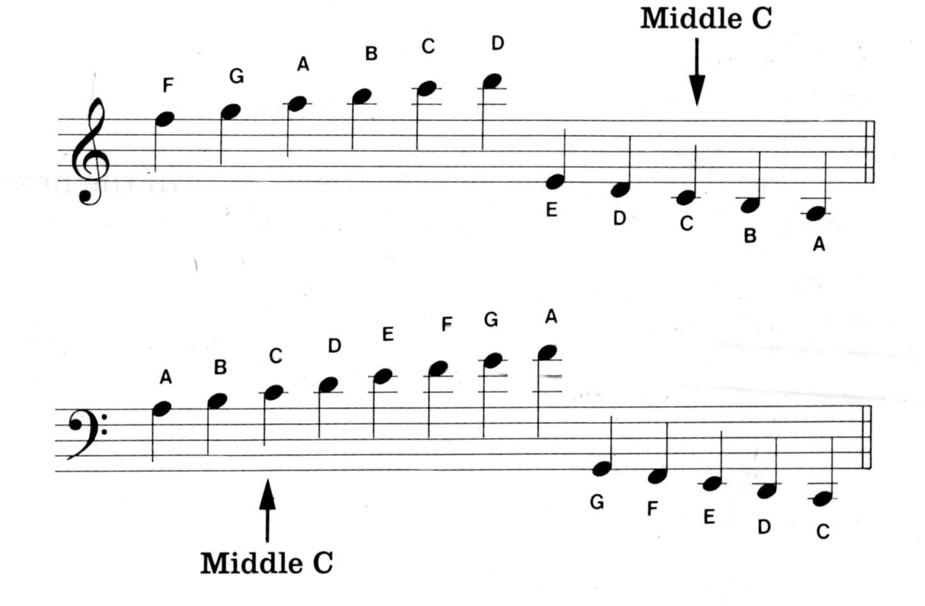

Lullaby
The groups of notes in the left hand of these pieces are called chords.
Chords sometimes need a little extra practice. Make sure you play all the notes at exactly the same time.
Lucy Locket

*These are the names used in North America.

# German folk song

# The train is a comin' in

## More about dynamics

*Piano (p)* tells you to play quietly.

*Mezzo forte (mf)* tells you to play fairly loudly.

*Forte (f)* tells you to play loudly.

f

# Singing tune

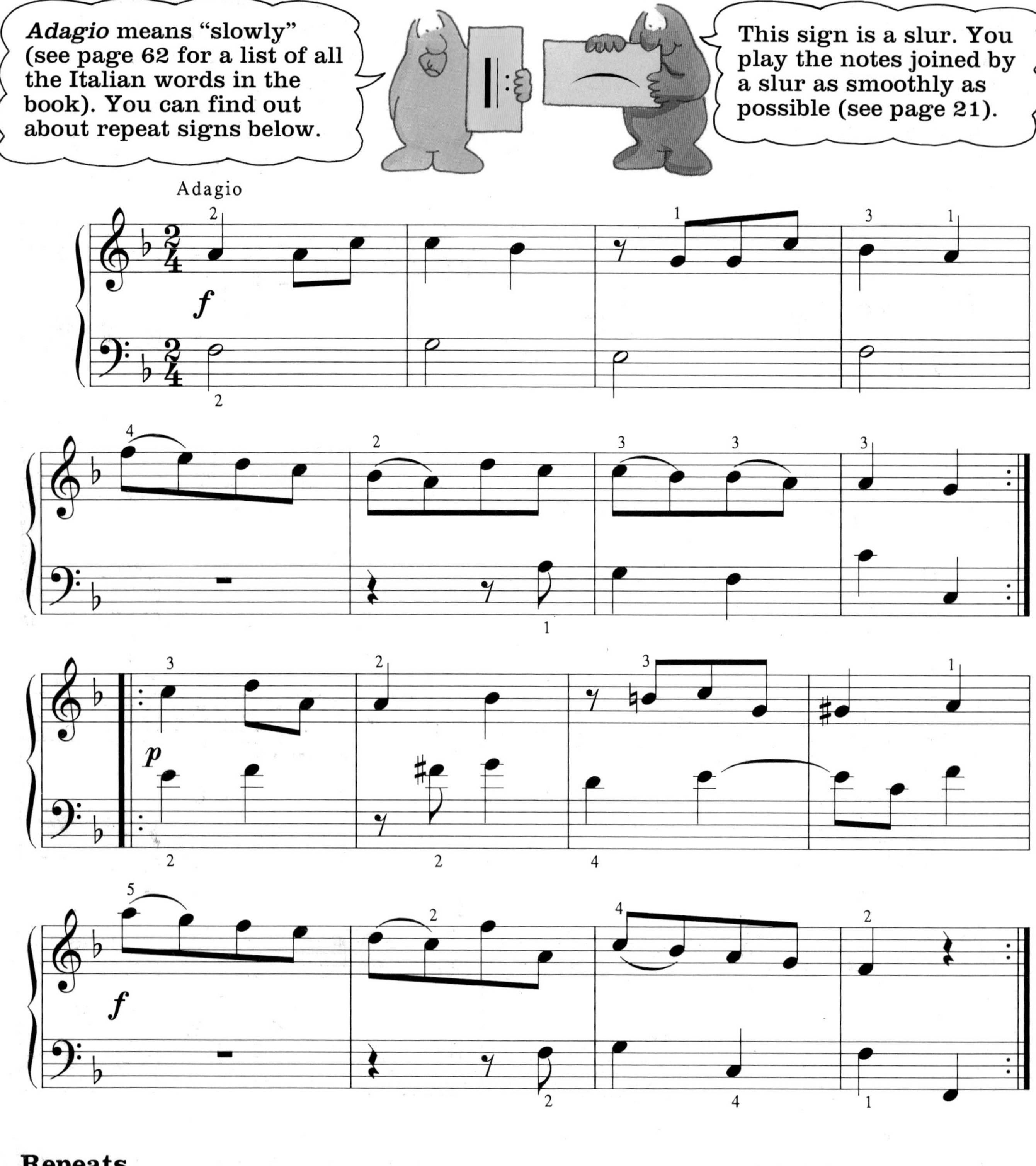


## Repeats

# Theme from the Trout Quintet

# Twinkle, twinkle little star

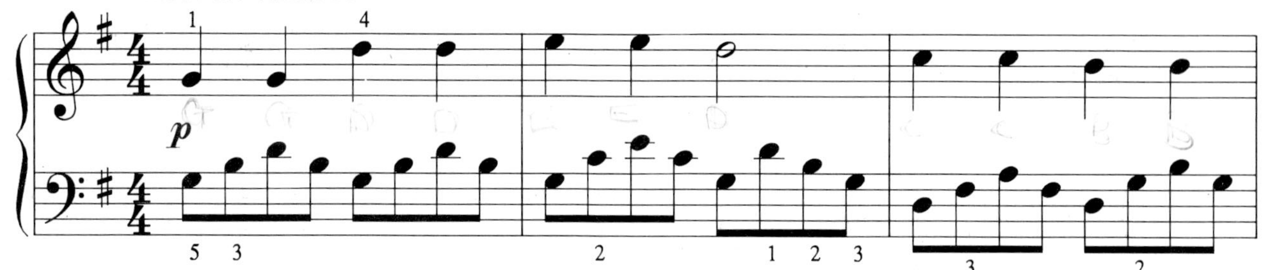


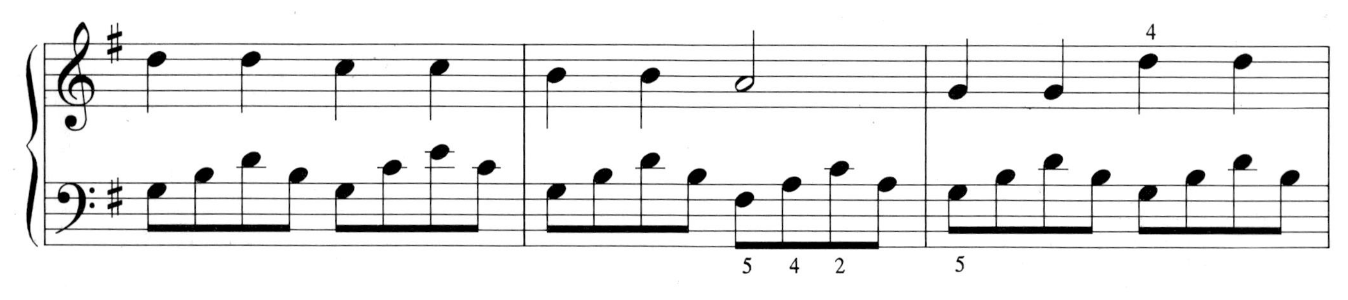


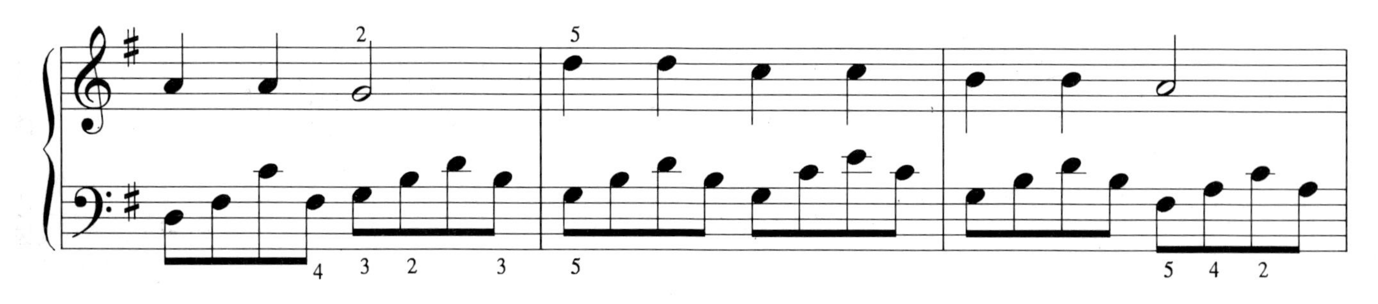

**Words for other speeds**

# Minuet

This tune is by the Austrian composer Wolfgang Amadeus Mozart (1756-1791).
The minuet is a dance in 3/4 time.

Andante
mp

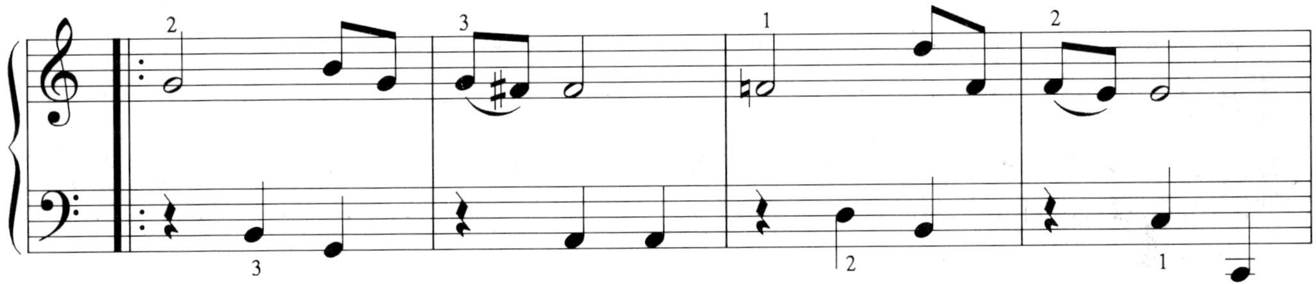

The minuet was very popular in the 17th century, at the court of King Louis XIV of France.
People danced to minuets on the tips of their toes, fairly slowly.

# Two by two

A curved line that joins two notes of the same pitch* is called a tie. To play tied notes press the key for the first note, and hold it until the end of the second note.

A dot after a note or rest means it lasts for half its length again.

* The pitch of a note is how high or low it is.

Warming up
Playing this tune will help your fingers warm up so that they work better when you play tunes.
Try to play this tune as smoothly as possible. Playing smoothly is called legato (see page 21).
Moderato
mf
Getting strong
This tune will help you to strengthen your fingers.
Play it slowly at first, and increase your speed gradually.
Moderato
mf

# March

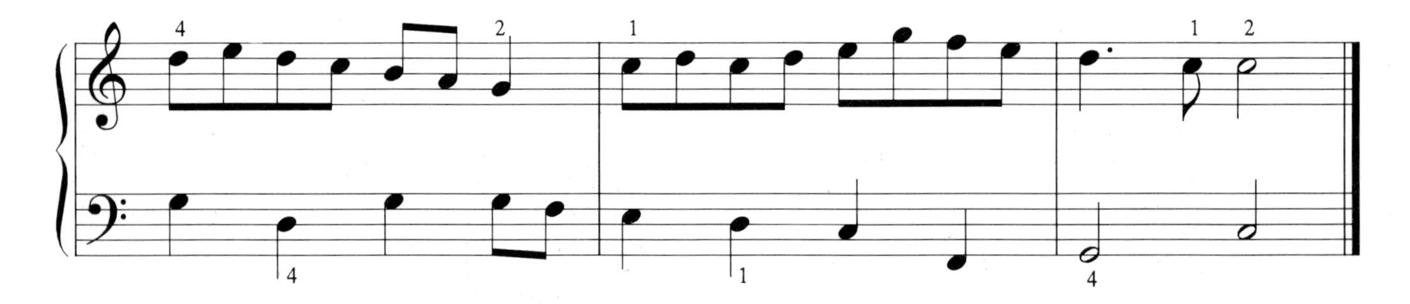

# English minuet

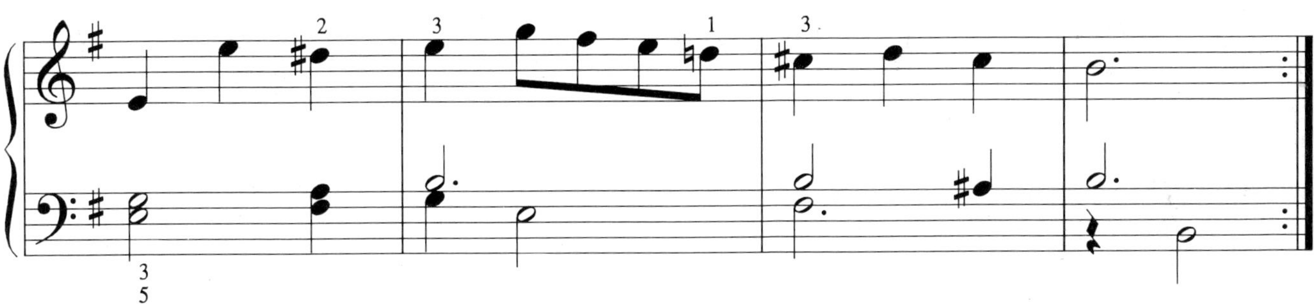

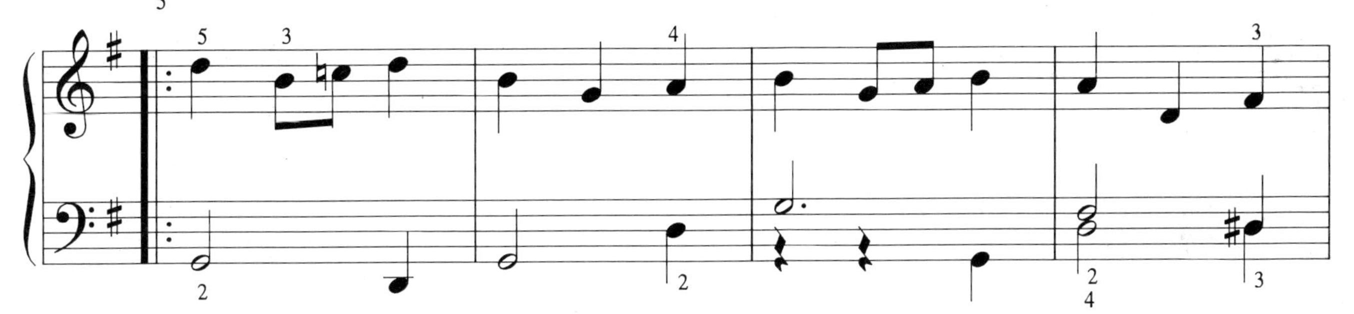

*Rit.* is short for *ritenuto*, which means "slow down".

# Cradle song

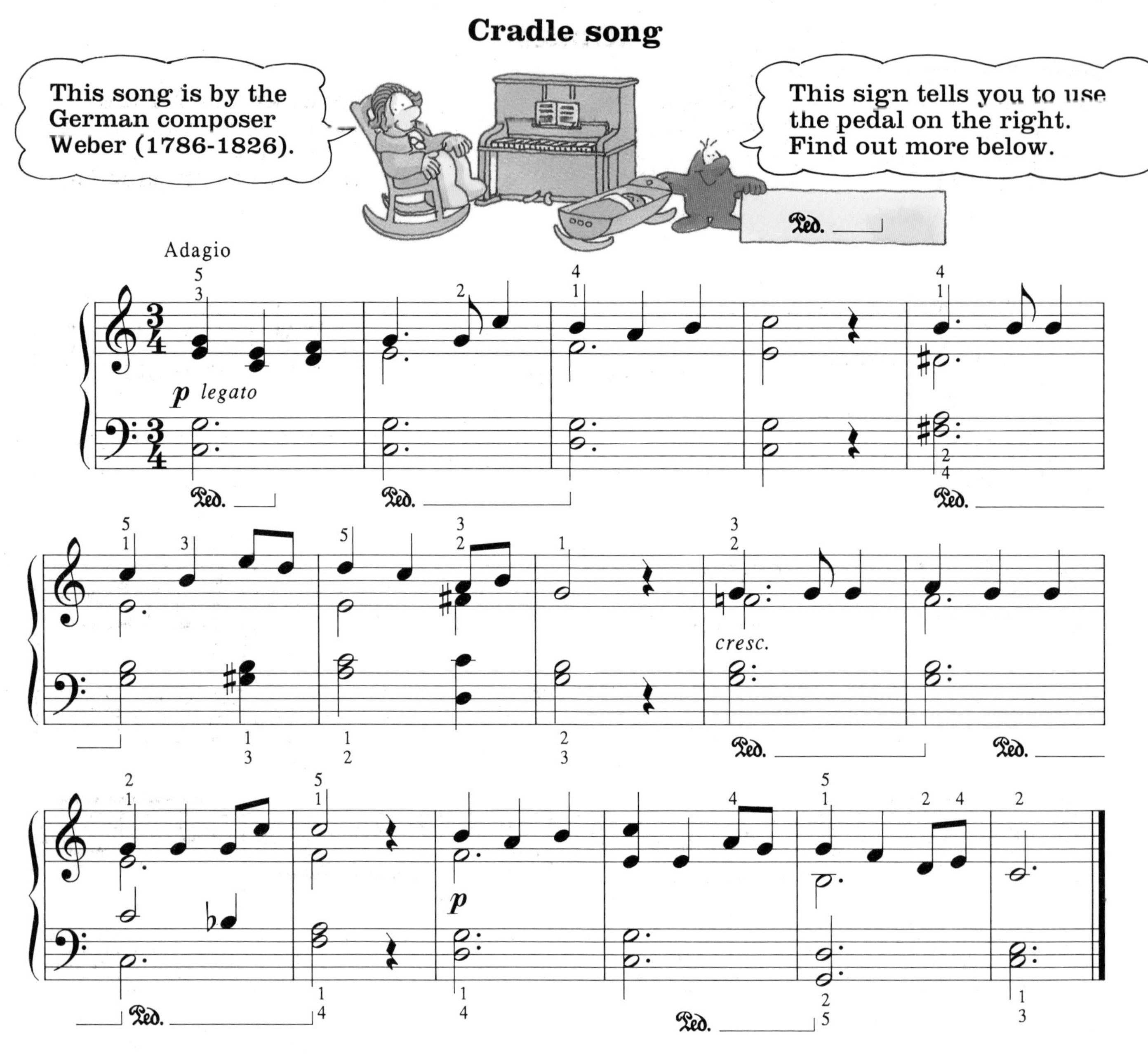


## Using the sustaining pedal*

On the piano, the pedal on the right is called the sustaining pedal. It helps you move smoothly between two notes or chords. When you press it, the notes you have played will continue to sound. This is called sustaining. You can then move to the next note without making a break in the music.

* You can find out more about the sustaining pedal on page 45.

# Minuet

It was written for the harpsichord. You can find out more about the harpsichord on page 29.

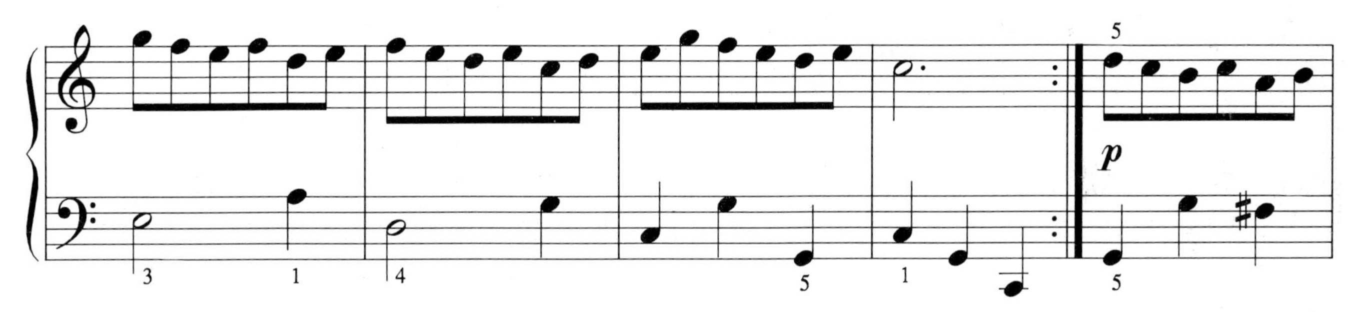

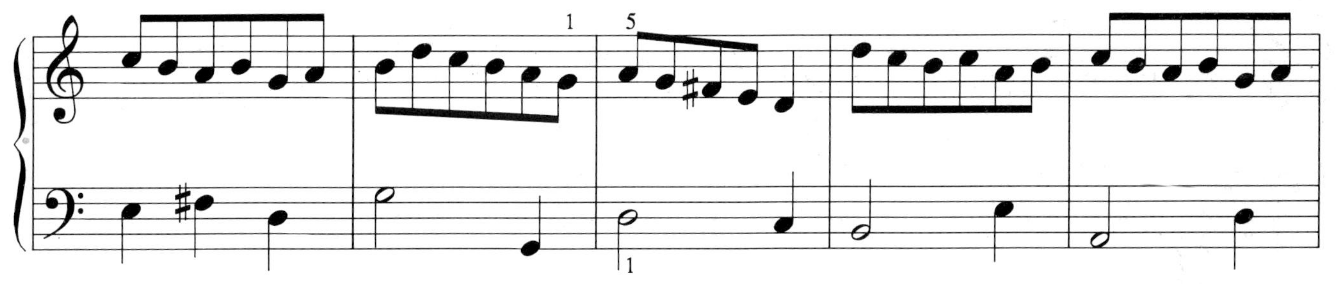

# Minuet

This tune was written by Leopold Mozart. He was the father of Wolfgang Amadeus Mozart, who wrote the tunes on pages 13, 34 and 52.

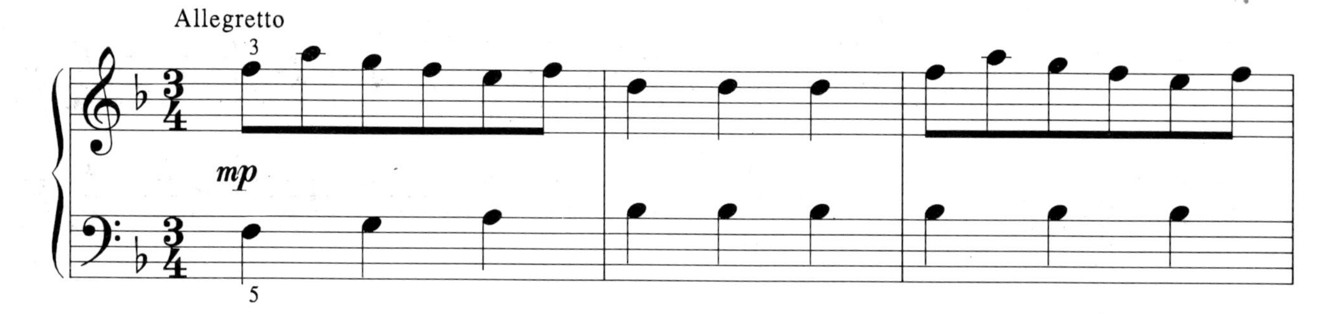

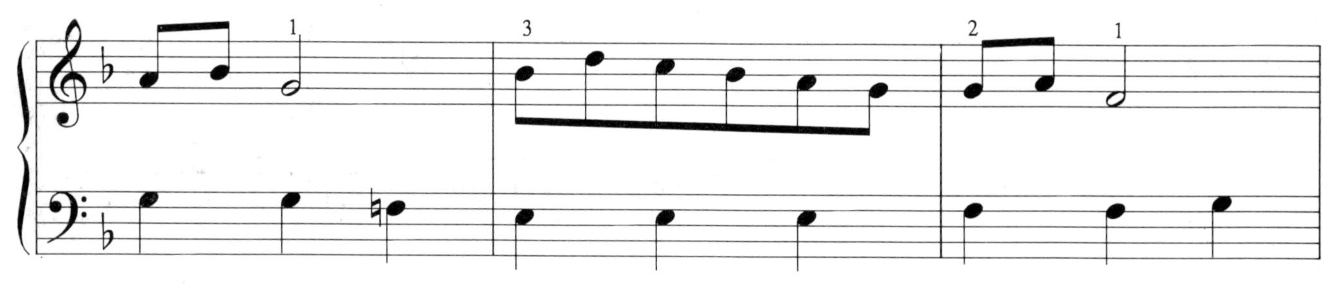

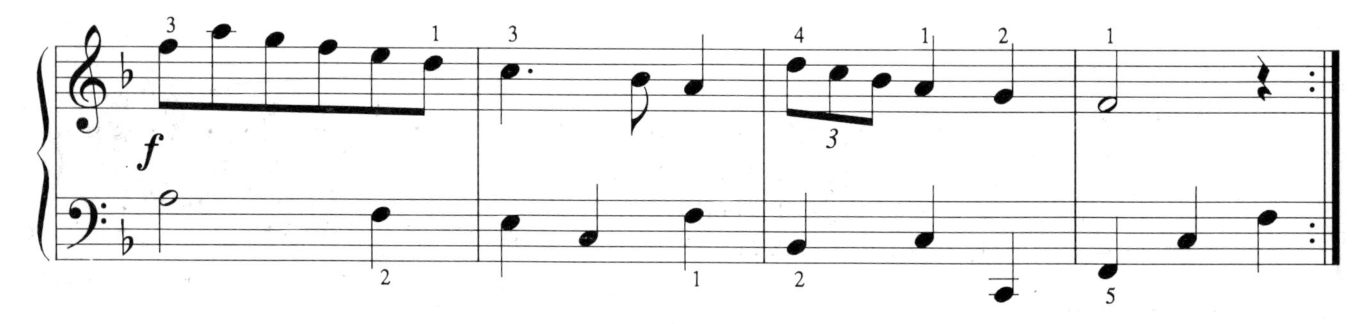

# Hymn tune

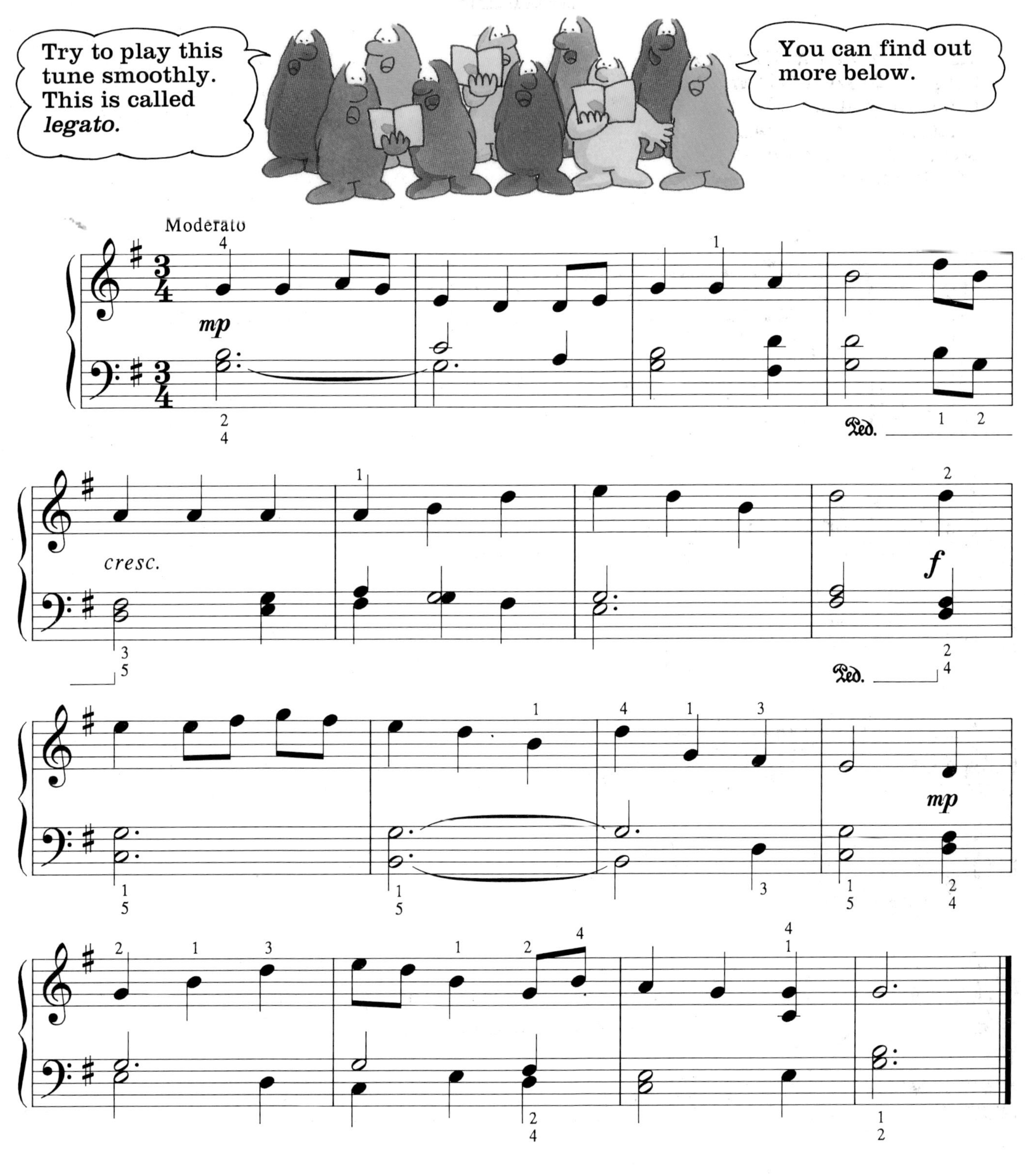


## Playing legato

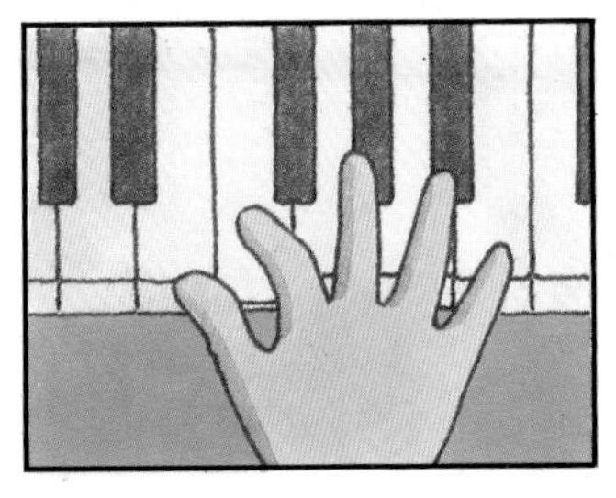

To play legato, you keep your finger down on one key until you press the key for the next note.

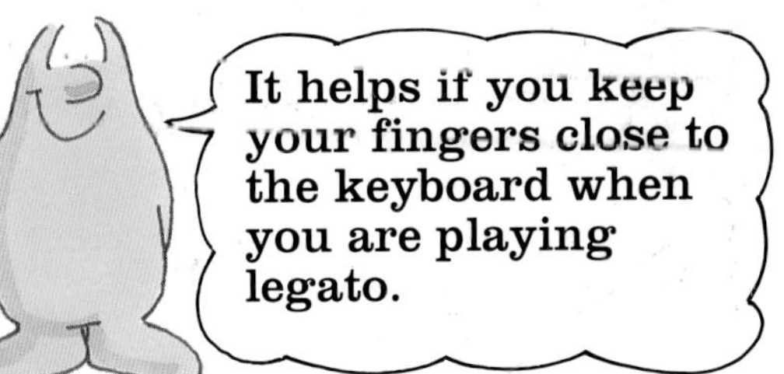

# The happy hare

This sign is a pause. You hold the note with the pause above it for about half its length again.

There is a special kind of repeat in this tune. Find out more below.

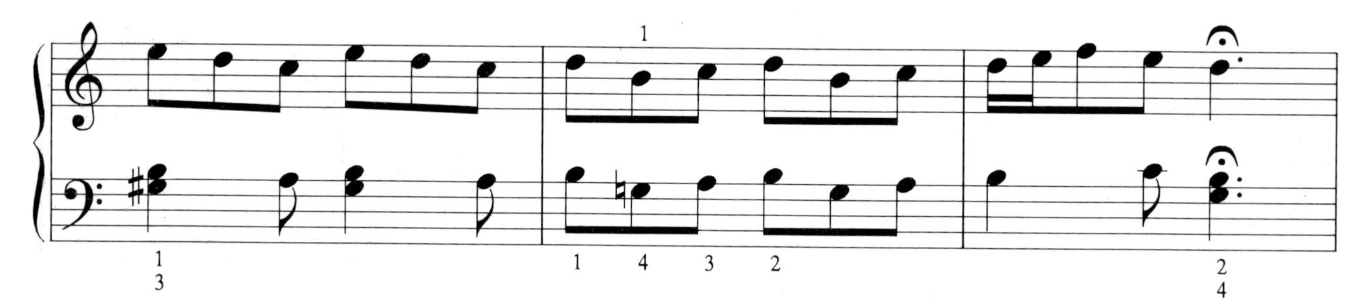

## First-time bars and second-time bars

# Burlesque

This tune is by Leopold Mozart.
A burlesque is a comical tune.
Allegro

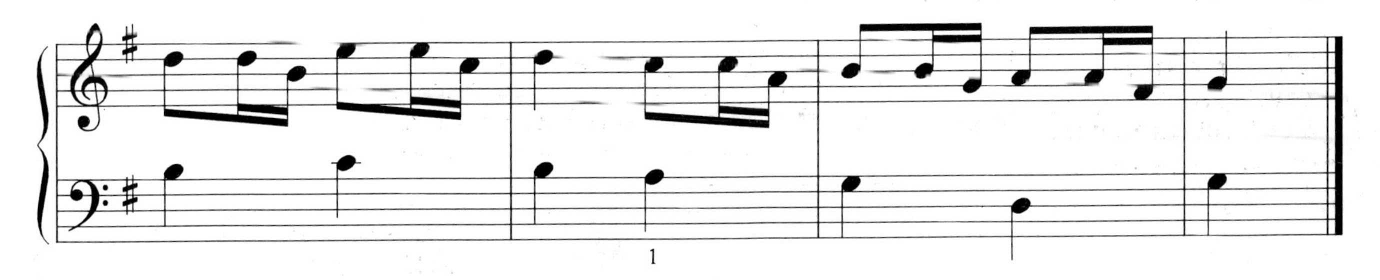

## Try, try, try again

### Accents and staccatos

To play notes with accents and staccatos, you press the keys a bit harder and more quickly than usual.

If you are playing a staccato note, you should also lift your finger as soon as possible, and make a break before the next note.

# Lilliburlero

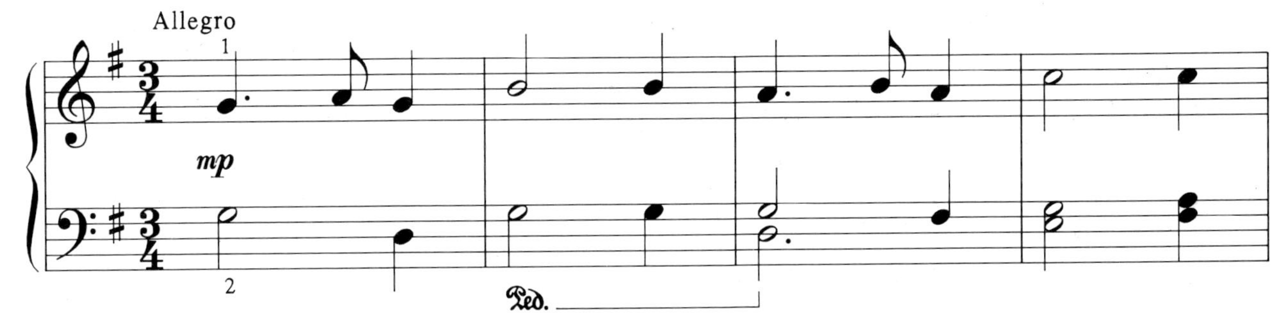


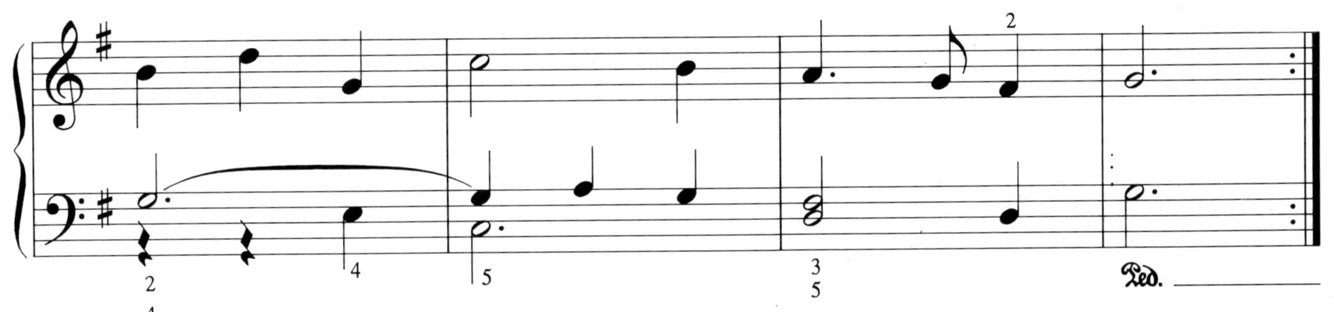

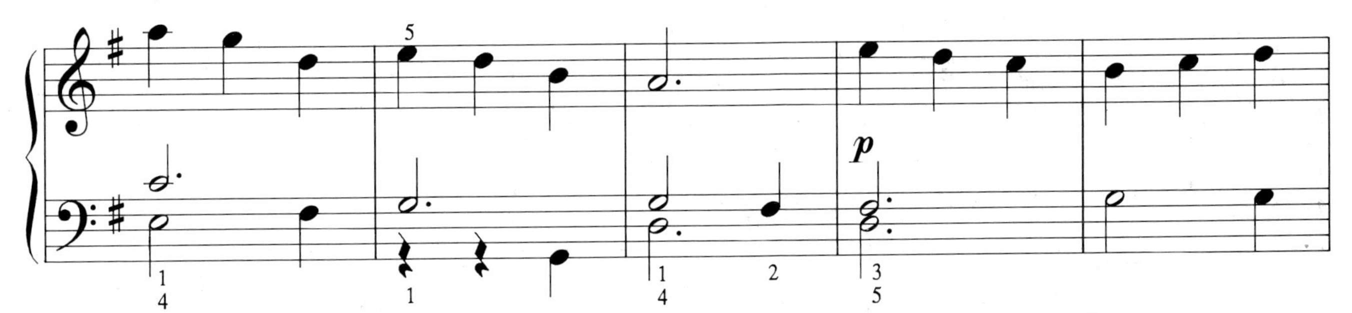

# Fanfare

**A fanfare is a short piece which is often played on trumpets. Fanfares are used for processions and celebrations of important people.**

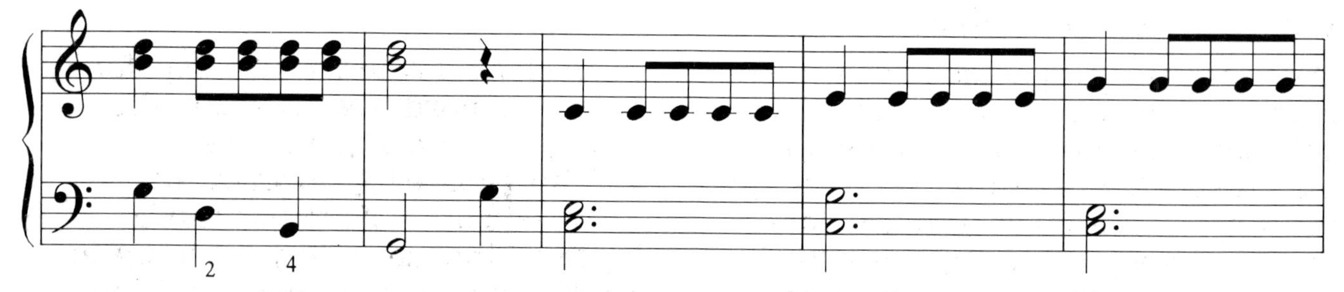

# Liza Jane

## Listening to piano music

Most famous composers have written music for the piano or earlier keyboard instruments such as the harpsichord. You can find recordings of many of these pieces in the library or record shop. Mozart (1756-1791) wrote lots of sonatas and concertos for the piano. Try listening to piano concertos no.25 and no.27.

Bach (1685-1750) wrote music for the harpsichord (see page 29), the organ (see page 47), and the clavichord (an early form of the piano). Some of this music can be played on the piano. Try listening to *The Well-Tempered Clavier* and the *Goldberg Variations*. You can find out more about piano music on page 32.

# Happy march

*Poco a poco diminuendo* means "get quieter little by little".
Use the weight of your arms and hands to play loudly. To play quietly, lift your arms a little.


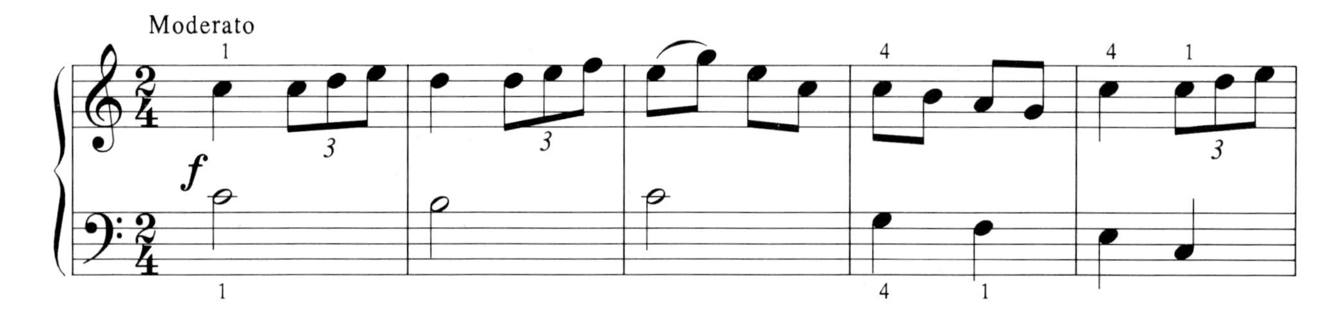

Moderato


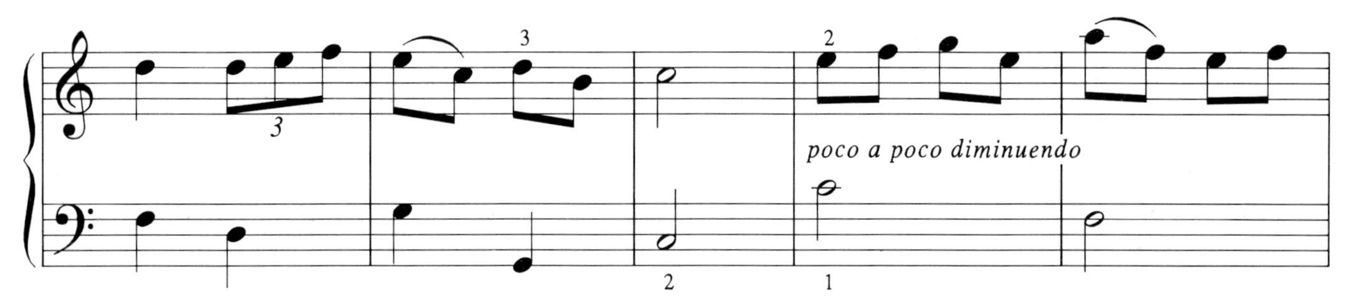

poco a poco diminuendo

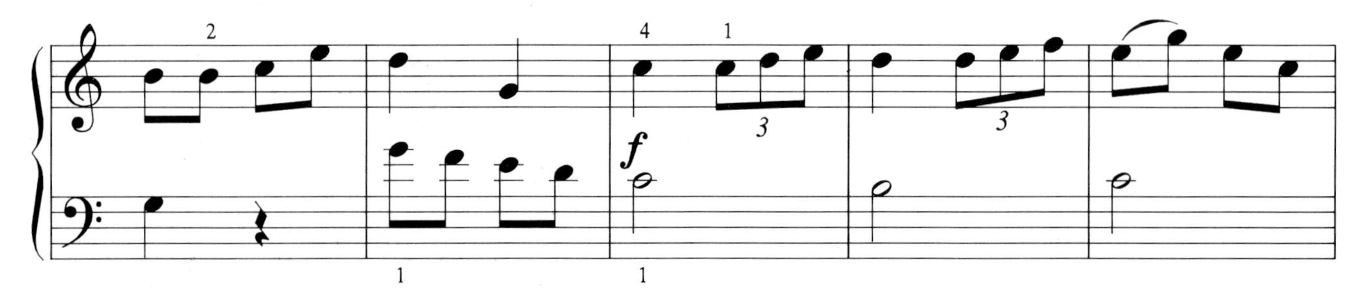

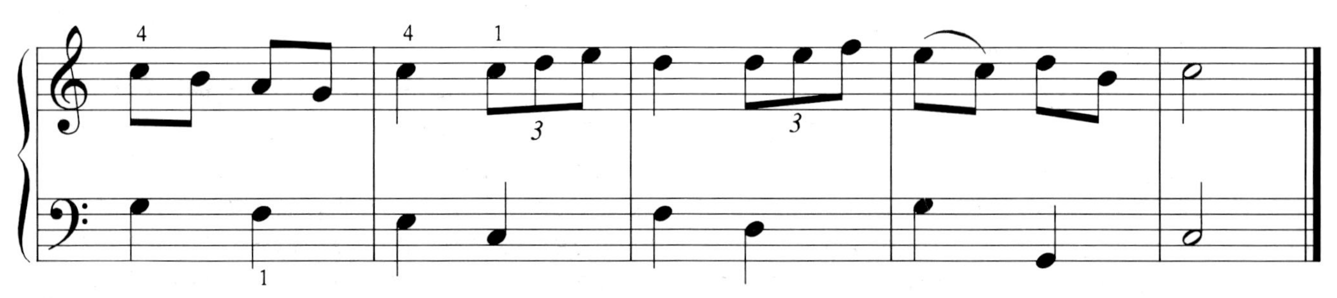

# The conquering hero

This tune is by Handel (1685-1759). It is from his oratorio *Judas Maccabeus*. An oratorio is a piece for a choir and an orchestra on a religious subject.

*D.C. al Fine* means you go back to the beginning and play the music again. Stop when you reach the word *Fine.*

## The harpsichord and the piano

The first harpsichords were built about five hundred years ago. The notes of a harpsichord are fairly quiet. Each key is linked to a piece of feather quill or plastic called a plectrum. When the keys are pressed, the plectrums pluck the strings.

When pianos were developed in the early 18th century, they became more popular than harpsichords. This is because they could play louder and longer notes than harpsichords, and because it was possible to vary the way the notes sounded.

The last rose of summer
This is an Irish folk song.
Adagio
mf
p
mf
dim.
p

# On the little hearth

# Lullaby

## Listening to piano music

During the 19th century, the piano became very popular. Composers such as Beethoven, Schubert, Schumann, Chopin and Liszt wrote lots of difficult music which was played in concerts by very good pianists called "virtuosi". Some also wrote shorter, more simple pieces for people to play at home. Schubert, who composed the tune on this page, wrote many piano sonatas and shorter pieces for piano such as *Impromptus*, *Moments musicaux*, and waltzes. He also wrote over 600 songs for voice and piano called *Lieder*, many of which have very good piano parts.

**The pianos that were built during the 19th century were bigger and louder than earlier pianos.**

**They could also play higher and lower notes than the pianos built during the 18th century.**

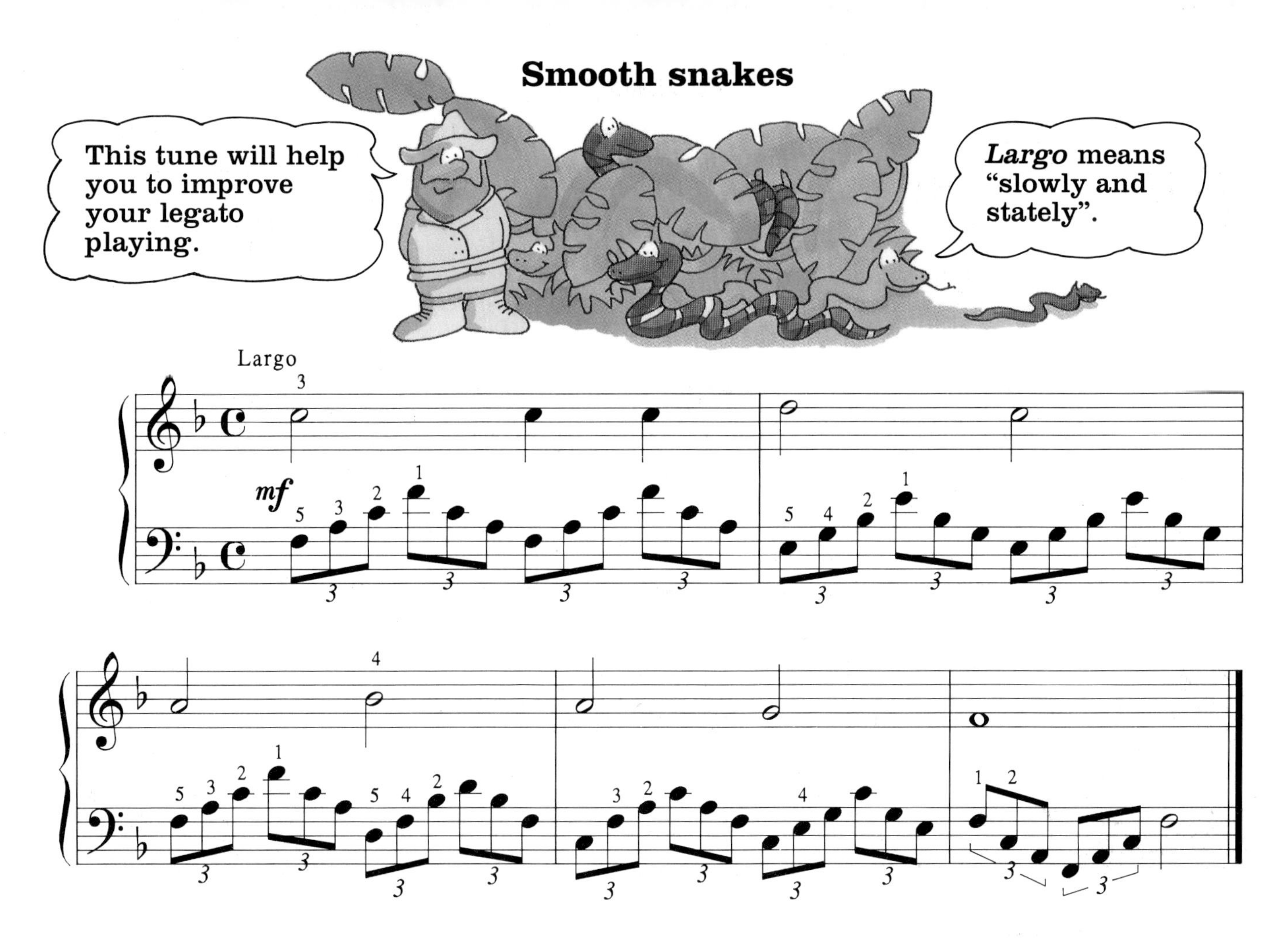


## Chords and arpeggios

The tune on this page contains arpeggios in the left hand part. Arpeggios are the notes of a chord which are spread out so that you play one at a time, either from the bottom up or from the top down. You can find out more about arpeggios and the scales that go with them on pages 50-51.

Sometimes chords are arranged to form a pattern called an alberti bass, in which the bottom note of the chord is played first, then the top note, then the middle note, and then the top note again. The alberti bass is named after Domenico Alberti, who often wrote bass lines like this.

# Là ci darem la mano

This tune comes from Mozart's opera *Don Giovanni*, which is based on an old Spanish story.

It is a sung by a man called Don Giovanni and a woman called Zerlina.

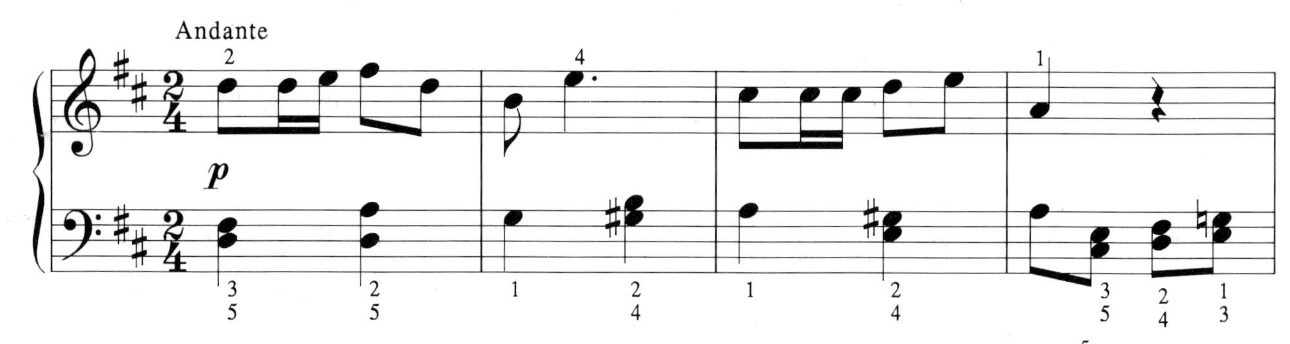

## Fingerings

The pieces in this book tell you which fingers to use. This helps you to place your hand in a position where you will be able to play all the notes. Many of the fingerings tell you to tuck your thumb under your hand. This helps you to change the position of your hand. Playing scales and arpeggios (see pages 50-51) will also help you to tuck your thumb under your hand.

# Minuet

This tune is by the German composer Bach (1685-1750), who came from a large family of musicians.

Bach wrote lots of music for the clavichord, the harpsichord and the organ. You can find out more about his music on page 27.

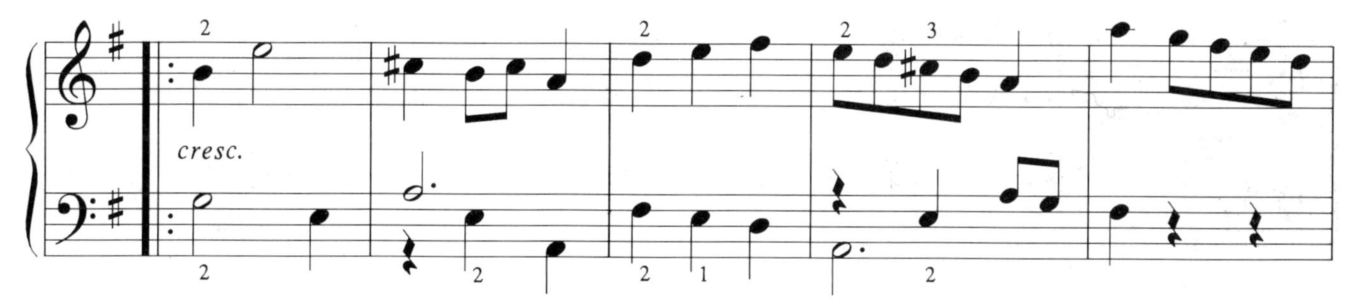


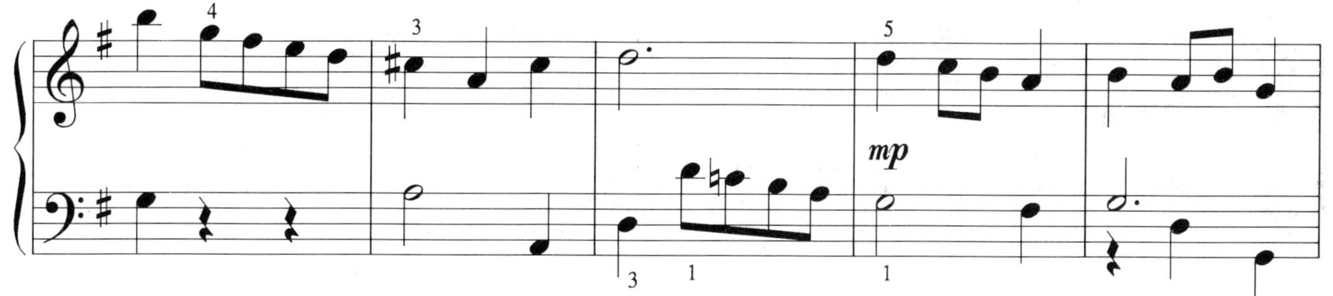

# Theme from Beethoven's Violin Concerto

# Air

This tune is by the English composer Purcell (1659-1695).

## Listening to piano music

On the next page there is some music by the German composer Schumann (1810-1856). Schumann was also a piano player and a writer on music. You could listen to his Piano Concerto in A minor, and to his pieces for solo piano such as *Papillons* and *Carnaval*. He also wrote some less difficult music called *Album for the Young*. The pieces on pages 38, 44 and 56 of this book are from *Album for the Young*.

# Humming song

When you see a note written as a quaver and a crotchet at the same time, hold the crotchet down for its full value, but keep the quaver line going as well.

This is another way of making you emphasize notes.

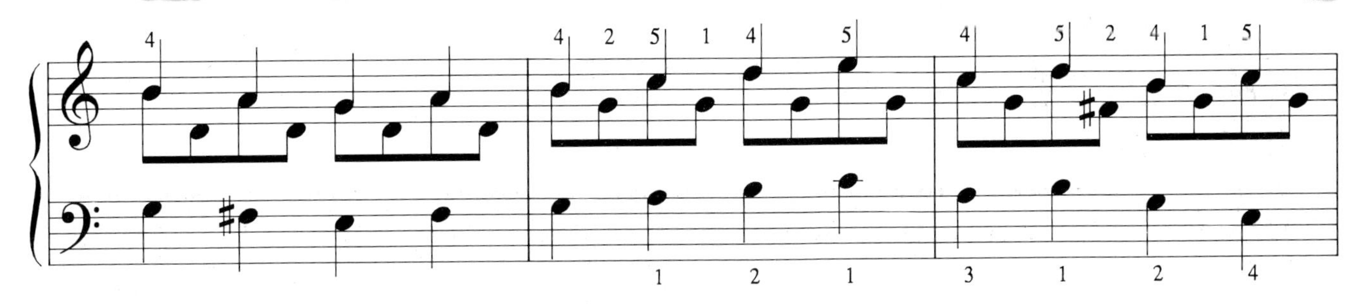

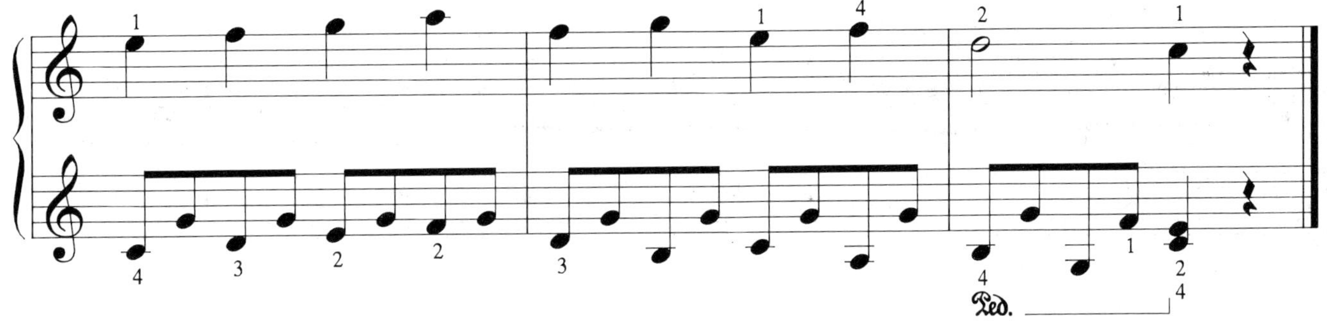

**Make sure you play the notes of the left hand line in the correct clef. They are in the treble clef at the beginning, but the clef changes twice during the piece.**

# Musette

This tune has a continuous note in the left hand called a drone. It imitates an old instrument called a musette, which was like bagpipes.

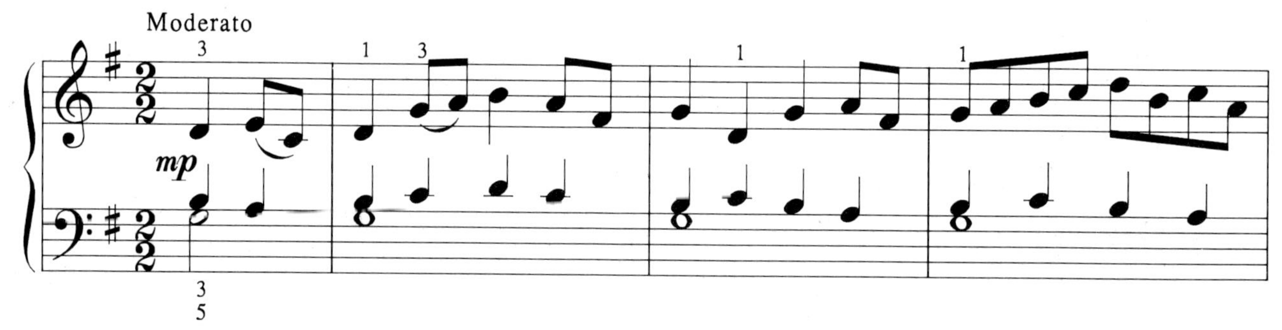

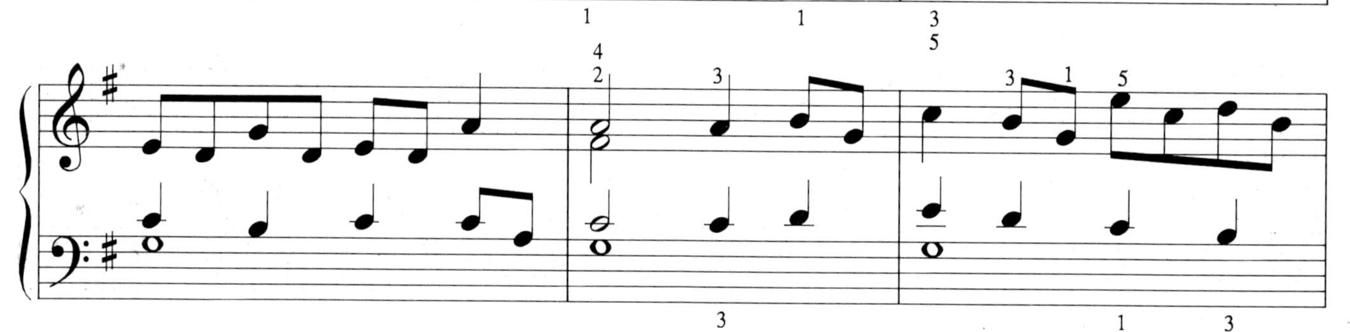

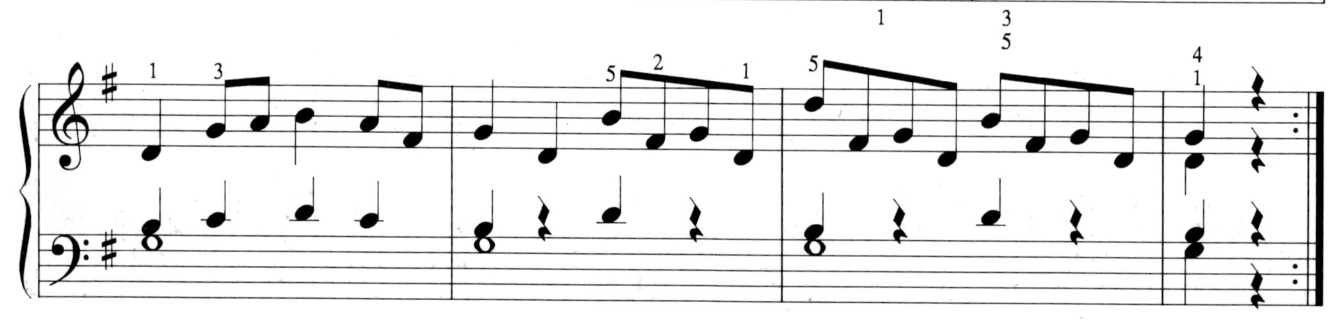

# Greensleeves

This is an old English tune. It is also known as *The Blacksmith.* The time signature means there are six crotchets in a bar.

## Pipe and drum

### Changes of time and key signature

Sometimes the time signature changes in the middle of a piece. In this tune it changes from four to three quavers in a bar. It will be easier to change time signature if you count the quaver beats in your head. This is because the speed of the quavers remains the same throughout the piece.

The key signature of a piece can also change. When this happens, a new key signature cancels the old one. In this tune, play F sharps before, and B flats after the change.

Blue study
The lines above and below the notes in the last line are called tenuto marks.
You can find out more about tenuto marks below.
Allegro
mf
cresc.
f
mf
Tenuto marks
To play a note with a tenuto mark press the key slightly harder than usual, and hold the note for its full value.
A tenuto mark is a way of telling you to emphasize a note.

# Melody

## Interpretation

Every performance of a piece of music is different. This is because there are many small changes you can make to alter the way the music sounds. You can play the music staccato, legato or a little faster, slower, louder or softer.

During your practice, try different ways of playing each phrase until you like the way it sounds. This is called interpretation. Interpretation gives your playing its own special character.

Schumann was married to a pianist and composer called Clara Wieck.

She knew many famous musicians, including Brahms (1833-1897).

### More about the sustaining pedal

Sometimes you can use the sustaining pedal even if it is not marked in the music.

You can use the pedal to play big jumps more smoothly.

Make sure that when you use the pedal, you only press it very gently.

# Paris Quartet

This tune is by the German composer Telemann (1681-1767).

This sign is a trill. You can find out how to play trills below.

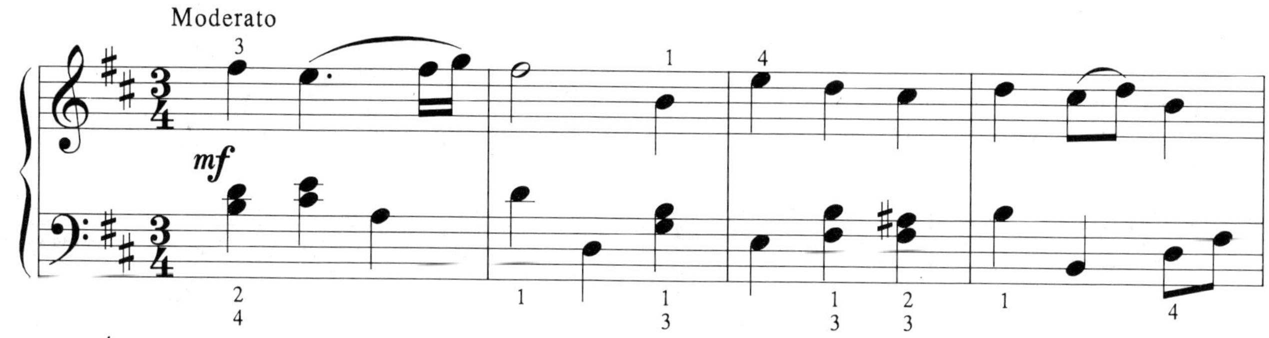


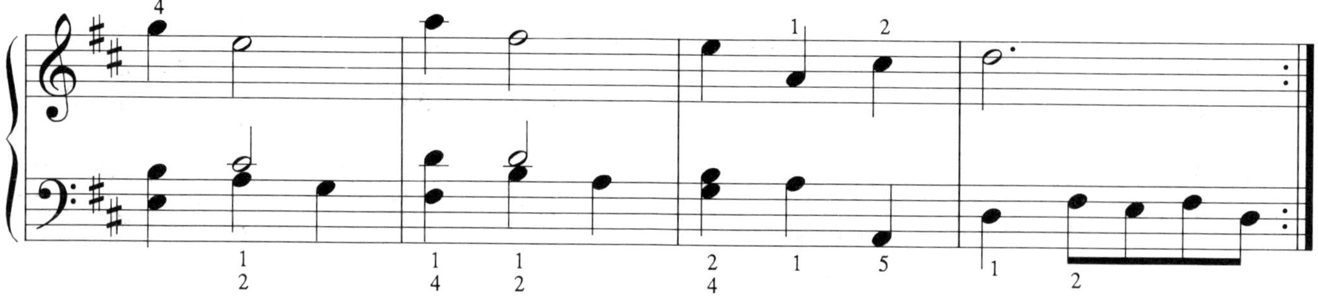

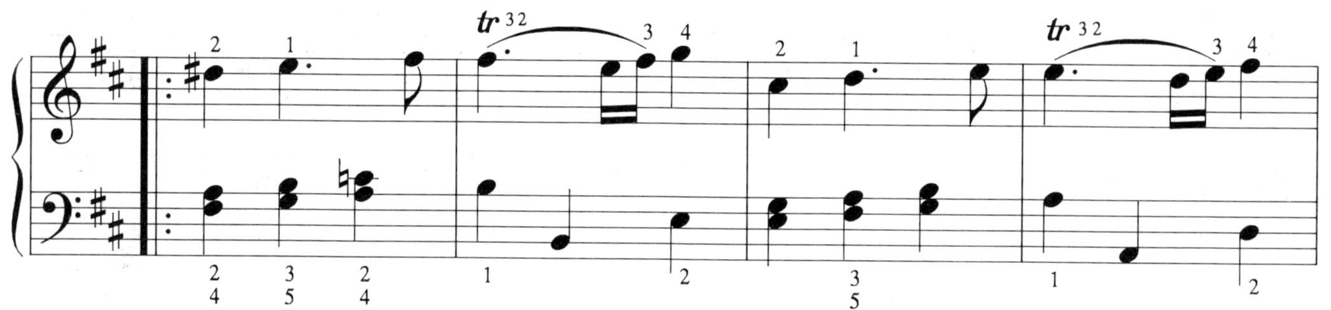


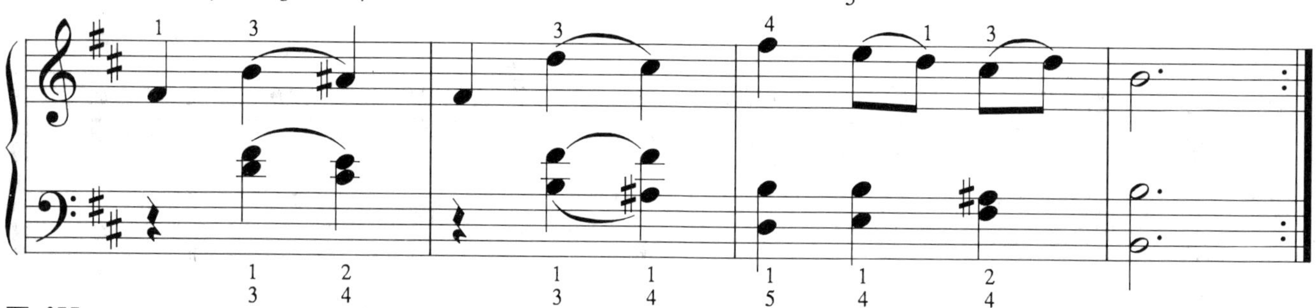

## Trills

To play a trill, you play the note on which the trill is written and the note above it (see below).

Alternate between the two notes for as long as the note with the trill on it lasts, like this.

tr =

# Chorale

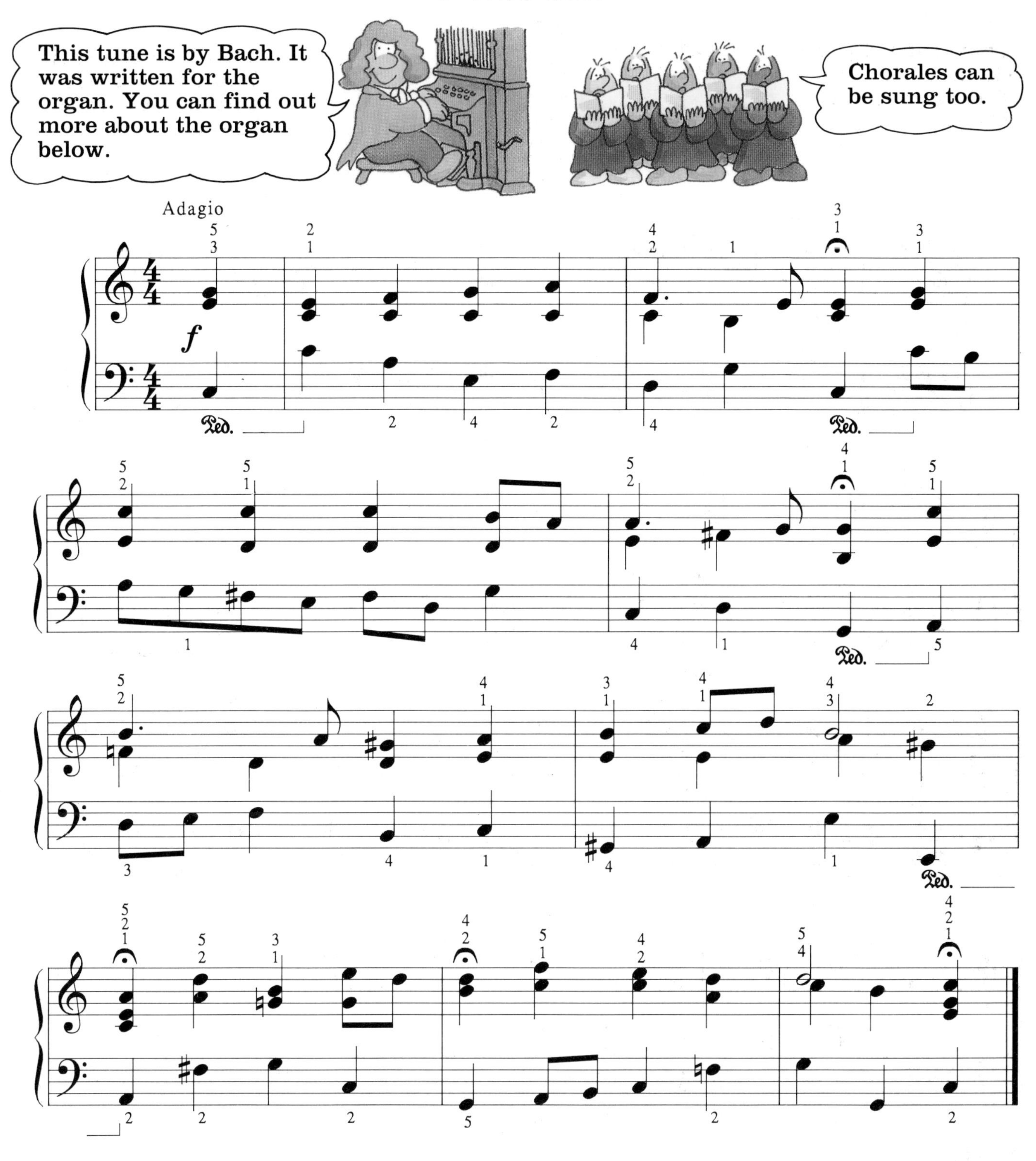


## The organ

The organ is the oldest kind of keyboard instrument. Its sound is produced by pipes of different sizes, made from metal and wood.

Bach was a famous organ player. He wrote lots of music for the organ. Some of it can be played on the piano.

# Minuet

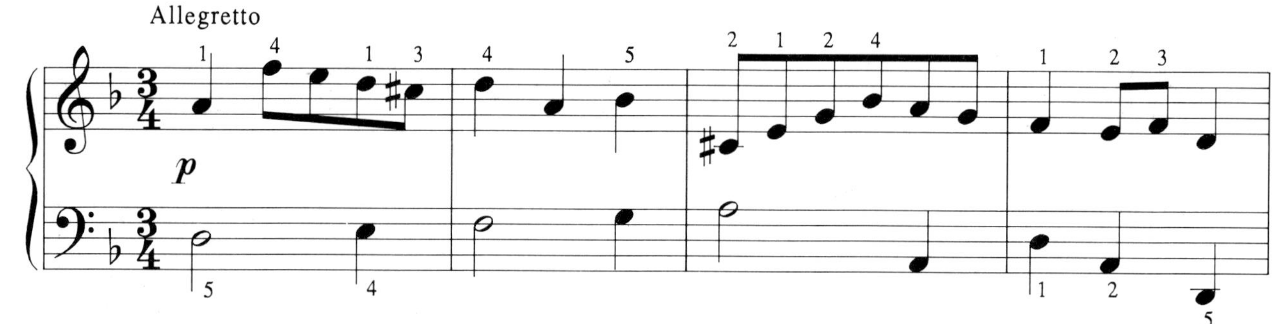


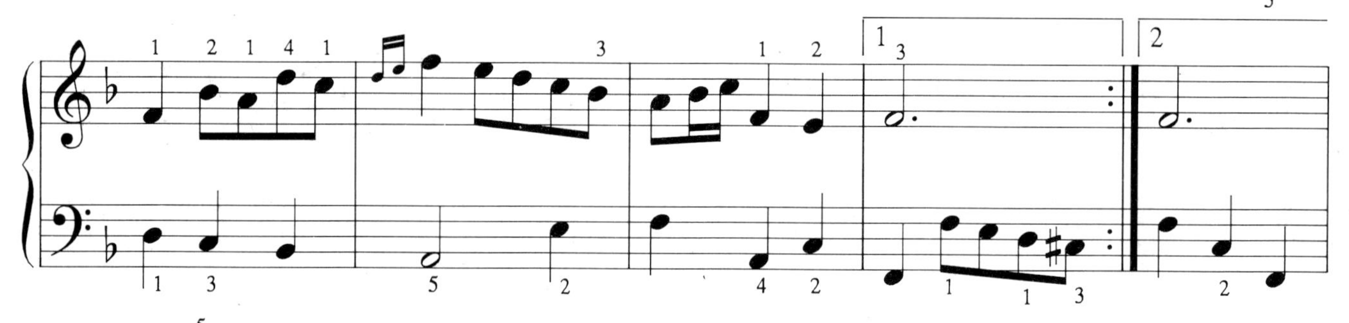

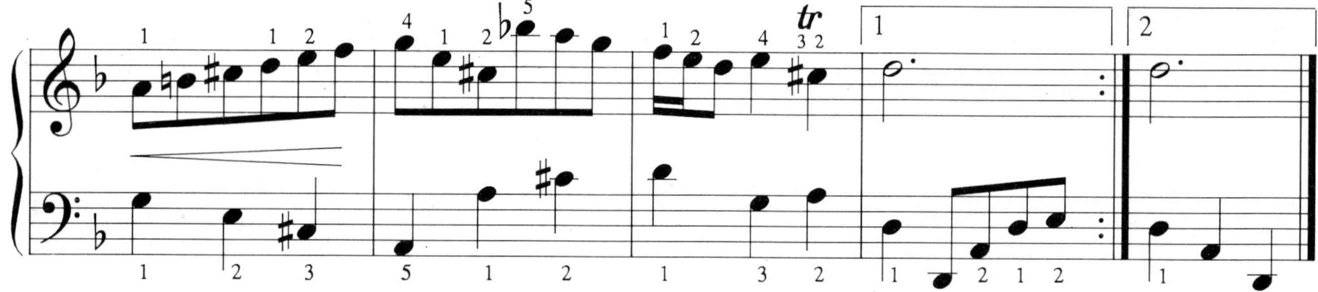


**Grace notes**

Grace notes decorate the music. Usually you play them just before the beat.

Don't play them too quickly.

# Summer song

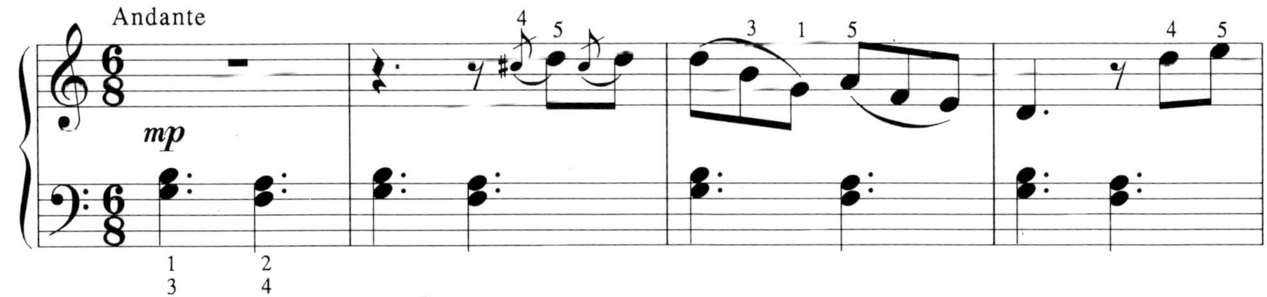


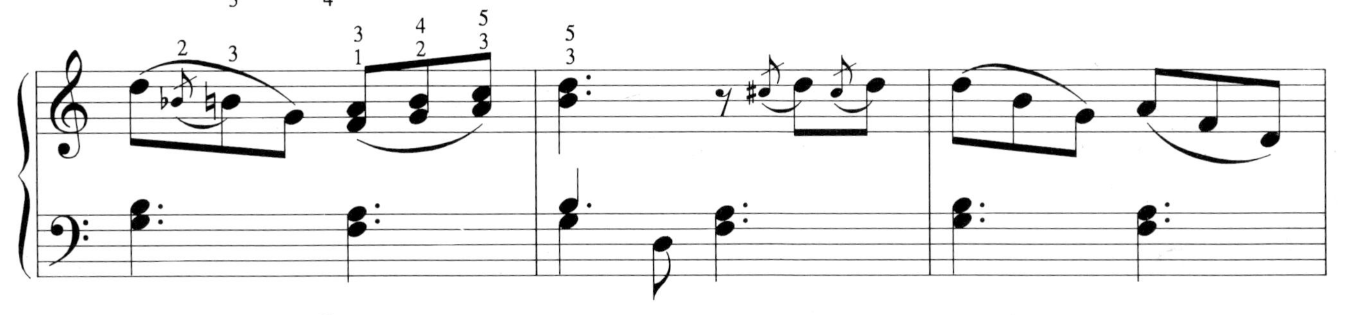

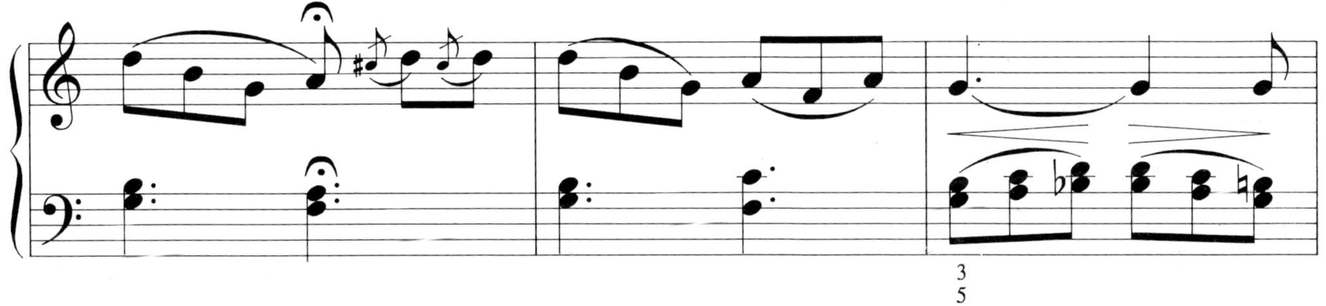

## Acciaccaturas

The word acciaccatura comes from an Italian word meaning “to crush”.

You play an acciaccatura as quickly as possible, before the note to which it is attached.

## Scales and arpeggios

Scales are chains of notes that go up and down by step. There are two kinds of step in a scale: whole steps (tones) and half steps (semitones). A tone is made of two semitones put together. There are several kinds of scale. One of the most common is the major scale. The order of the tones and semitones in every major scale is the same. The steps between the third and fourth notes, and the seventh and eighth notes in a major scale are semitones. All the other steps are tones.

Arpeggios are spread chords. You can play them at the beginning of your practice, with the scale of the same key. The notes of an arpeggio are the first, third, fifth and the eighth notes of the scale in the same key.

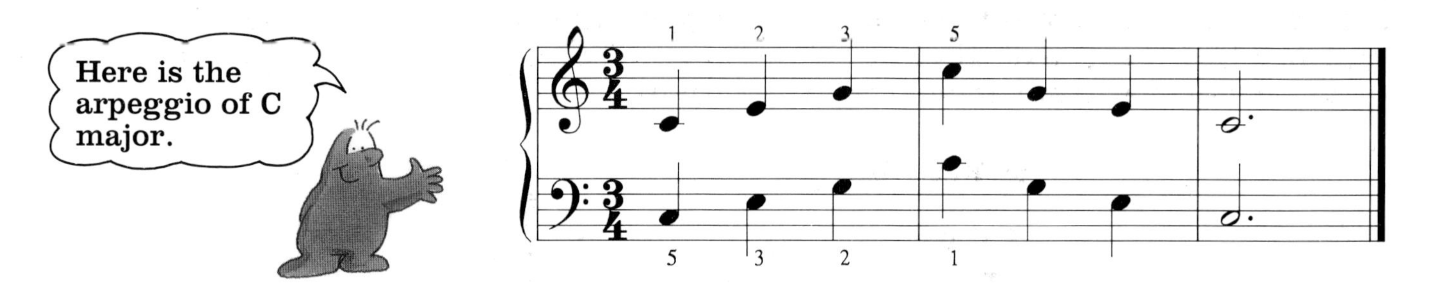


## Scales and arpeggios of more than one octave

The scales on page 50 are one octave long. An octave is the distance between one note and the next note above or below it with the same name.

When you play scales and arpeggios, repeat them a few times by starting at the bottom of the piano and moving up through several octaves.

# Rondo

In a rondo, the first tune you hear comes back several times during the piece, with new tunes in between.

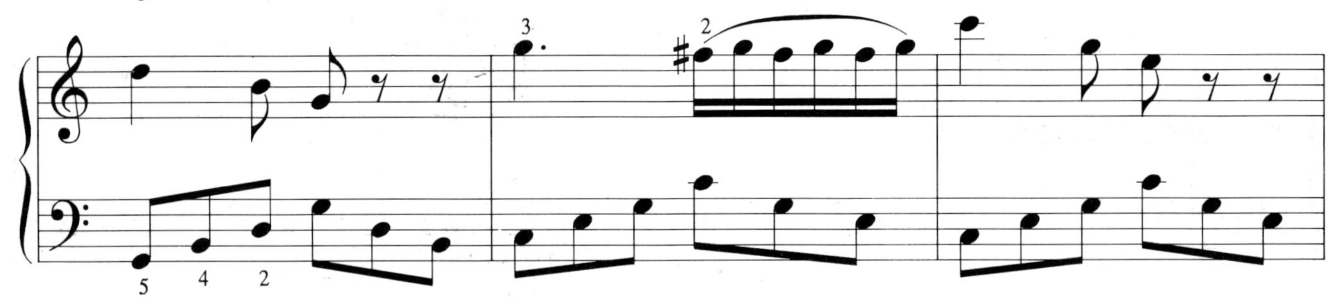

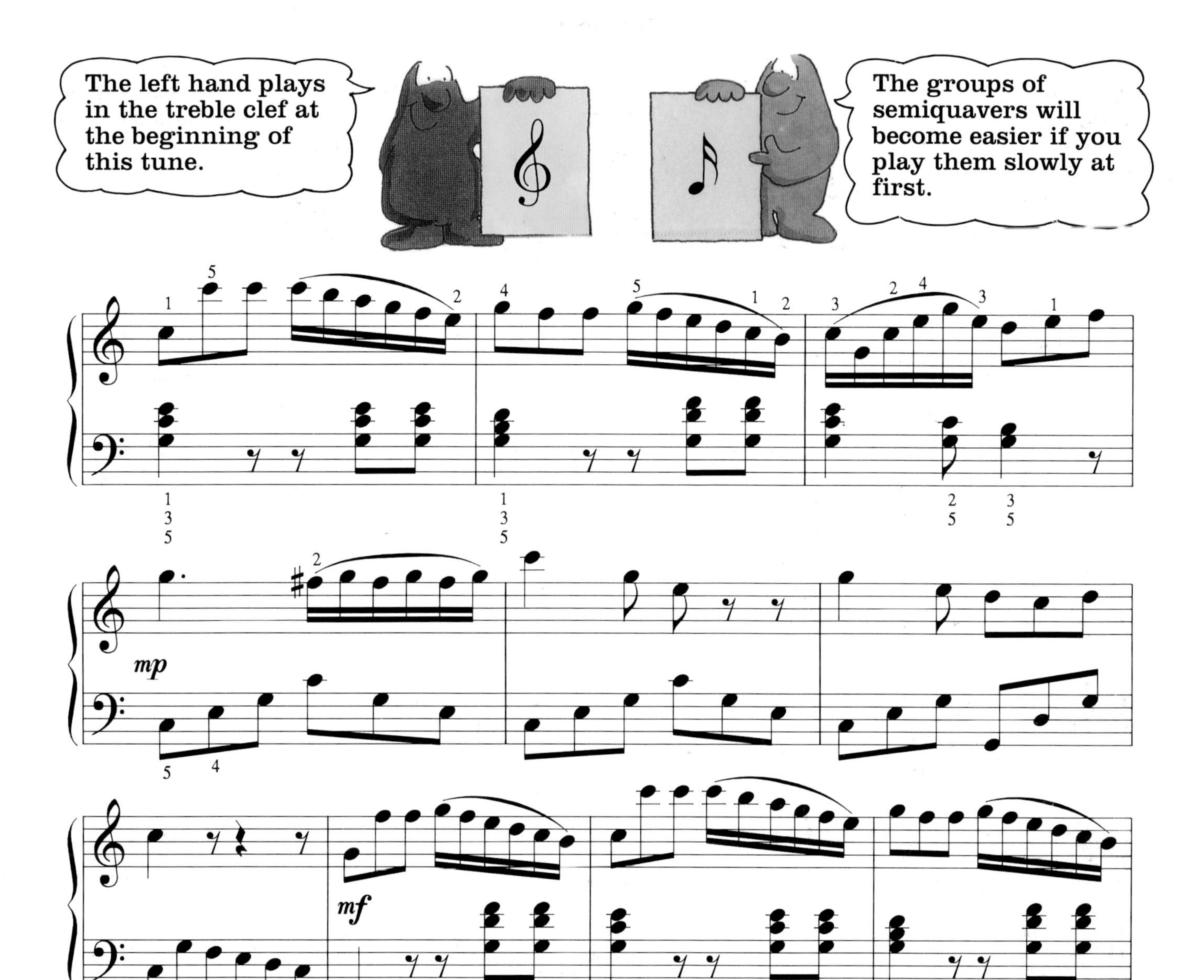
The left hand plays in the treble clef at the beginning of this tune.
The groups of semiquavers will become easier if you play them slowly at first.
mp
mf

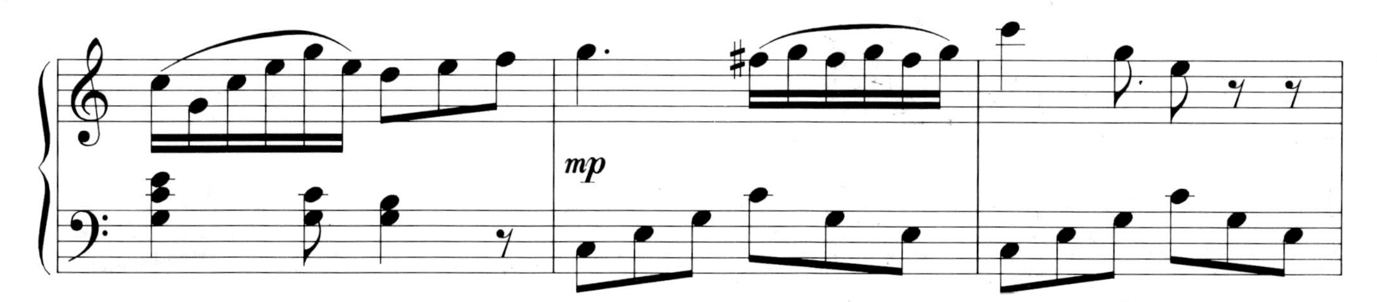
mp

dim.
f

# Waltz

This tune is by the Russian composer Tchaikovsky (1840-1893). There are E sharps in the third line. E sharp is the same as F natural.

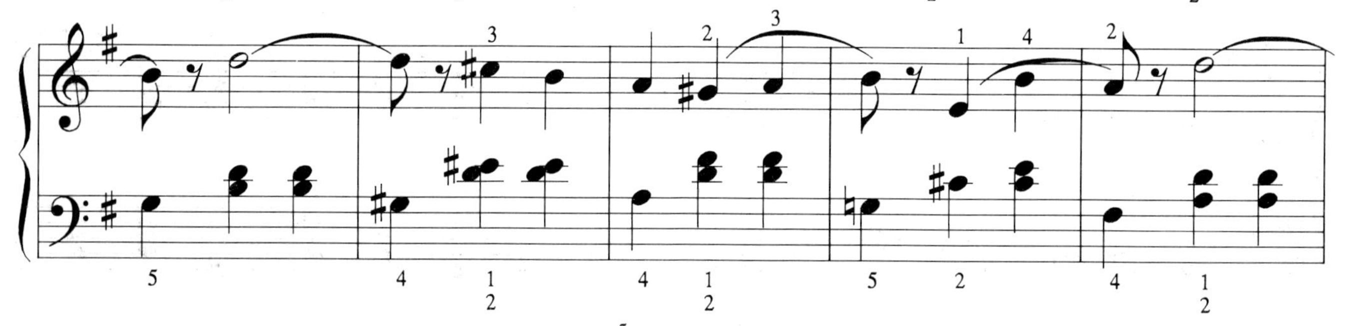

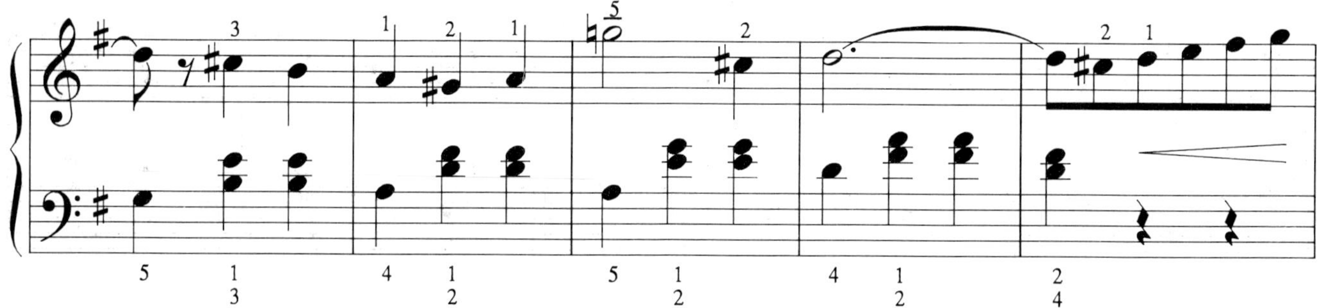

Tchaikovsky also wrote lots of famous music for ballets.

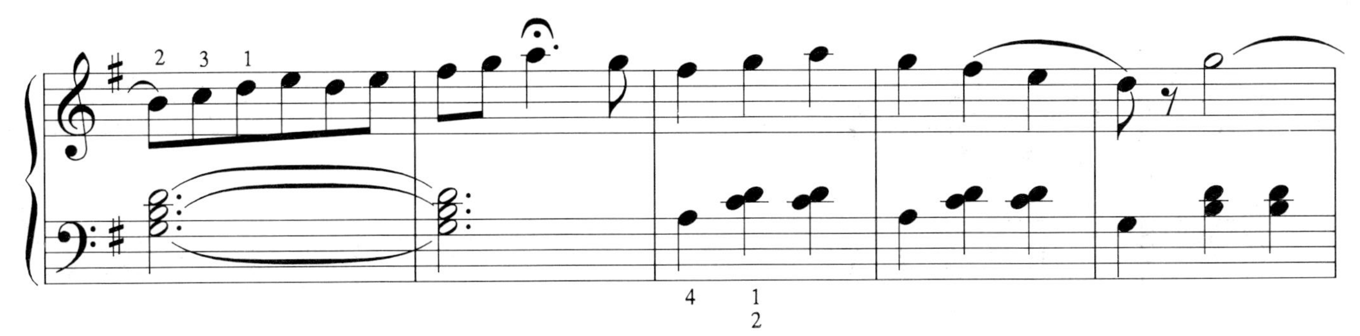

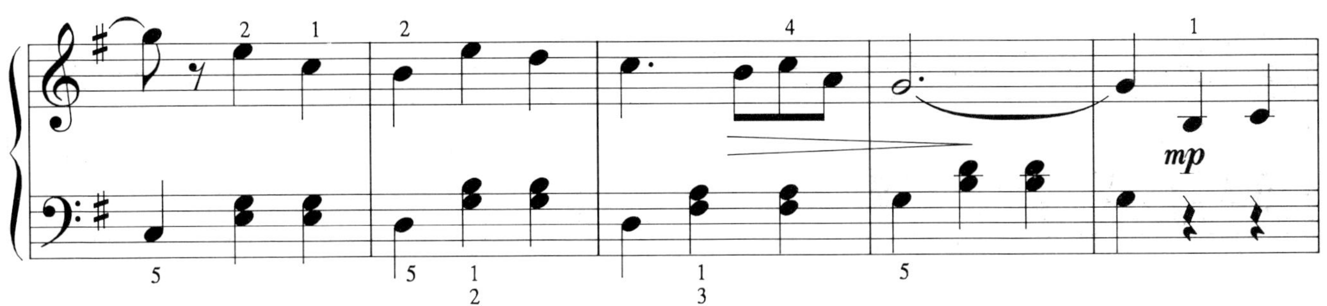

# Song of the reapers

# Polonaise

This tune is by Bach. It is from the book of music he wrote for his wife Anna Magdalena.
The polonaise was first danced in Poland during parades and processions.

Andante
mf

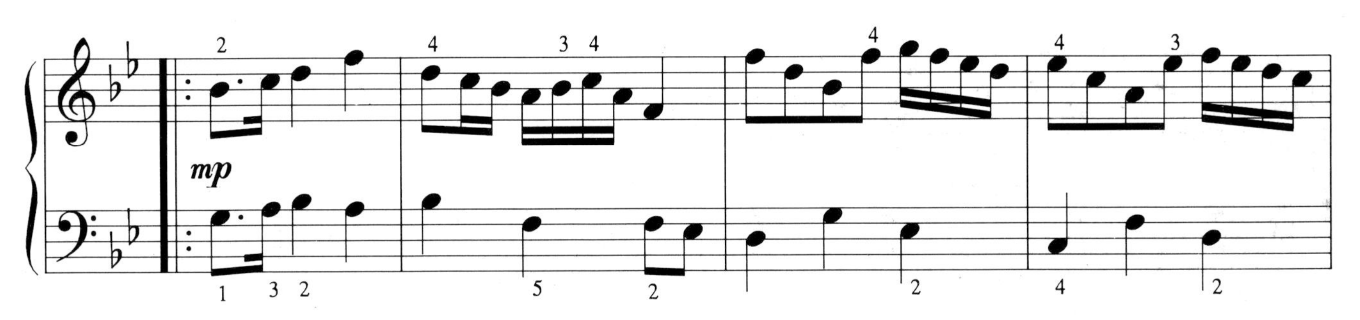
mp

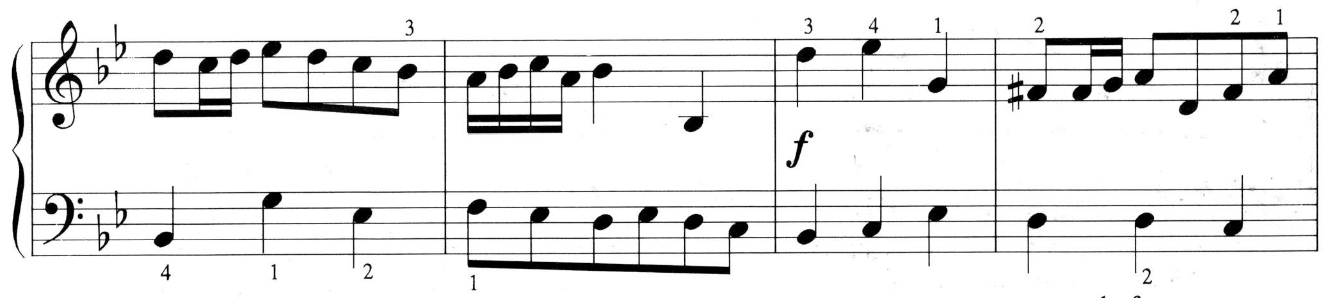
f

p
cresc.

In this tune you could try playing the quavers in the right hand part staccato, and the semiquavers legato.

# My vineyard (part B)

Part B is played by the person at the lower end of the piano. Part A is played by the person at the top end of the piano.

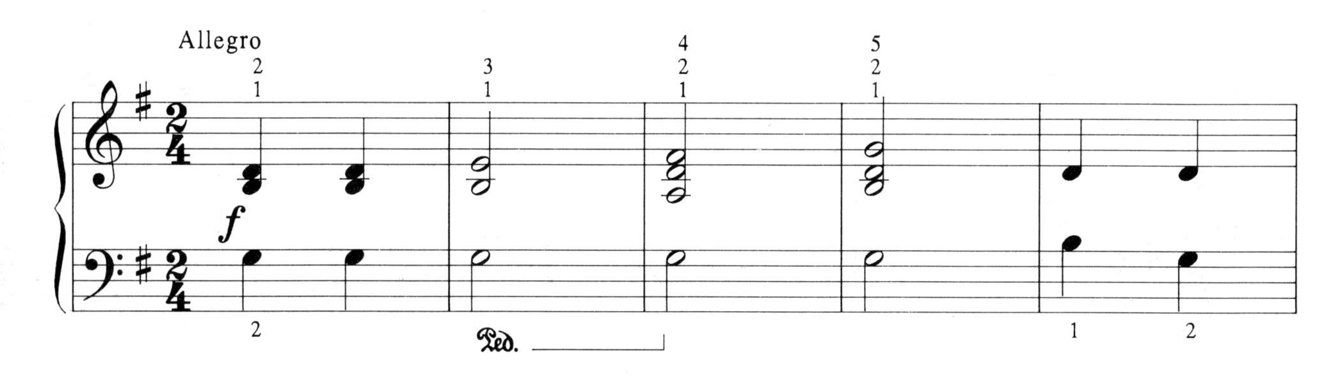


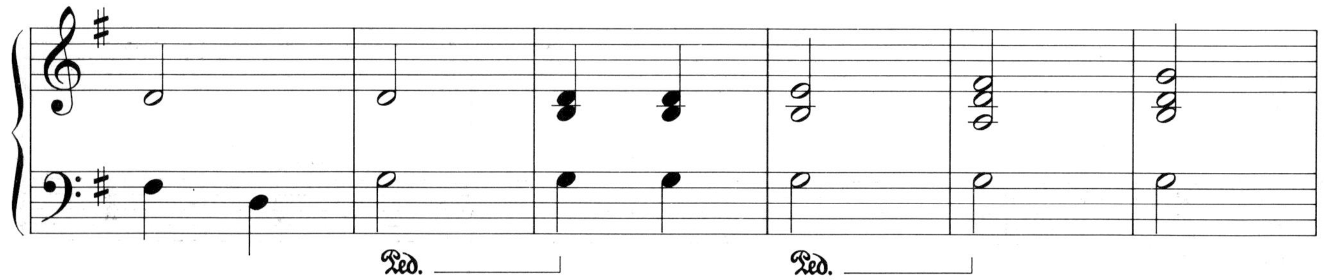

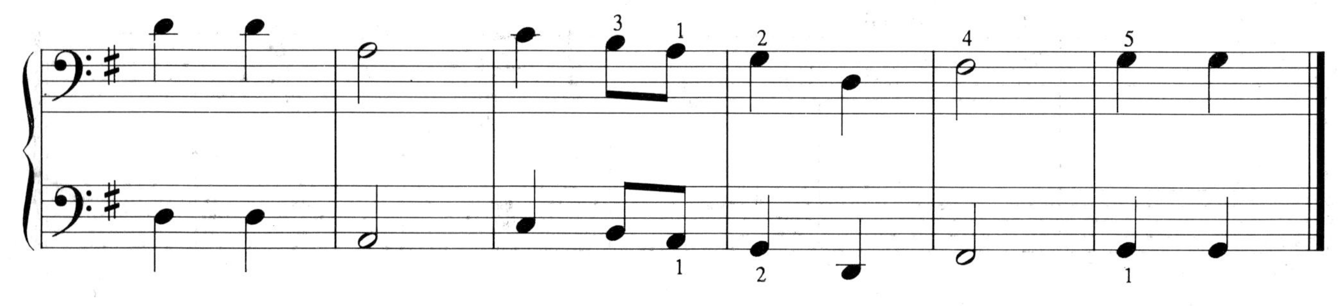

# My vineyard (part A)

It helps if you count a bar together before you start.

When you play duets, listen to the other person so that you play together exactly in time.

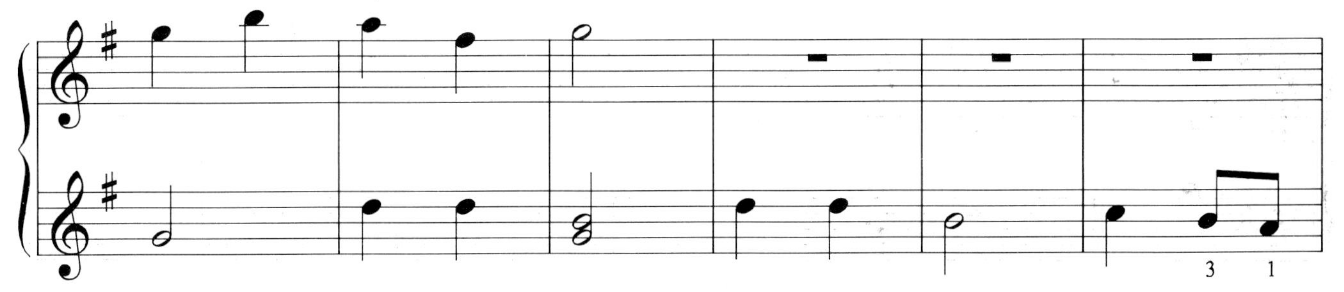

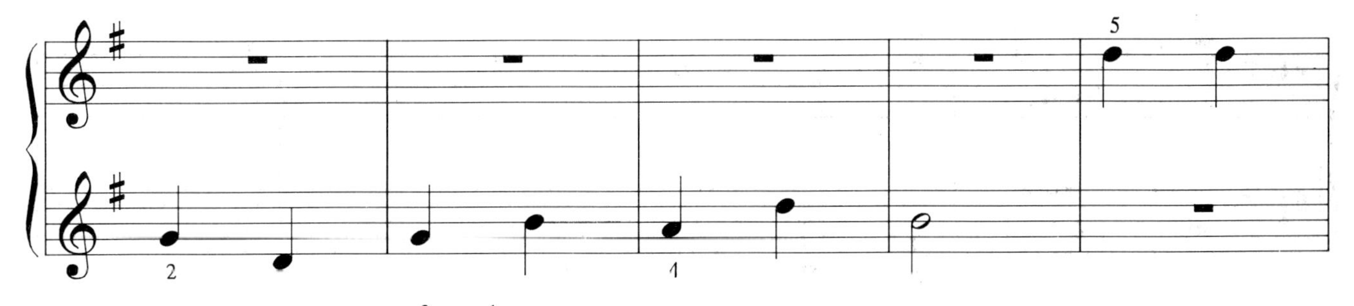

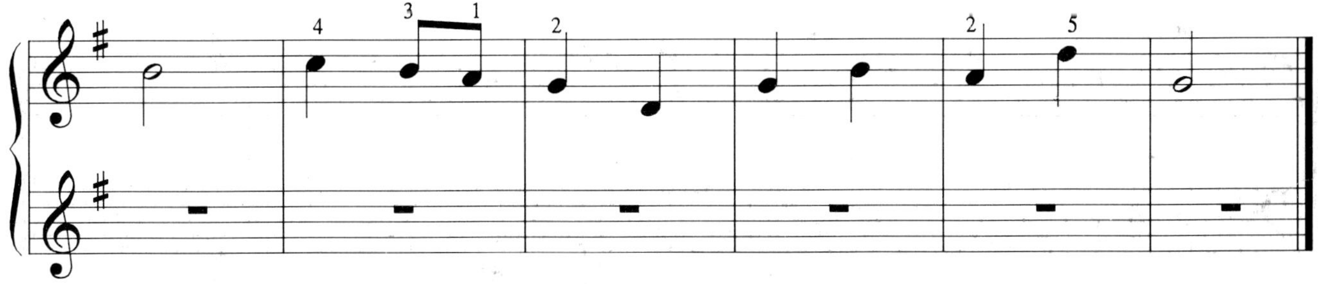

Humoresque (part B)

Humoresque
(part A)
A humoresque is a lively, but also slightly sad tune.
Dvořák wrote eight humoresques for piano.
Poco lento e grazioso
p leggiero
cresc.
dim.
p
mp
Fine
rit.
cresc.
dim.
cresc.
dim.
D.C. al Fine

## Music help

### Italian terms

This list explains the Italian words used in the book.

*adagio* – slowly
*allegretto* – fairly quickly
*allegro* – quickly
*andante* – at a walking pace
*cantabile* – singing
*crescendo (cresc.)* – getting louder
*D.C. al Fine* – back to the beginning, to *Fine*
*diminuendo (dim.)* – getting softer
*forte (f)* – loudly
*grazioso* – gracefully
*largo* – slowly and stately
*legato* – smoothly
*leggiero* – lightly
*maestoso* – grandly
*mezzo forte (mf)* – fairly loudly
*mezzo piano (mp)* – fairly quietly
*moderato* – at a moderate speed
*pesante* – heavily
*piano (p)* – quietly
*poco a poco* – little by little
*poco lento* – fairly slowly
*ritenuto (rit.)* – held back
*staccato* – short
*tenuto* – held

### Key signatures

The key signature of a tune tells you which notes to play sharp or flat. Here are some of the key signatures used in the book.

C major

G major

D major

F major    B♭ major

### Practice

At the beginning of your practice, you should warm up with some scales, arpeggios and exercises. If you come across any difficult bars when you play tunes, try them slowly. You could also invent exercises to help you with the difficult bars, such as playing them with a new rhythm or with staccato and then legato phrasing. When you go back to the original music it will seem easier, and then you can gradually increase your speed.

When you play, always choose a speed that you can manage without making too many mistakes. As you get to know the music you will be able to play faster if you want to.

### More music to listen to

Here is a list of music for piano that you might enjoy listening to.

Bach: *Goldberg Variations*
Mozart: Piano Concerto no.19
Beethoven: *Emperor Concerto*
Schubert: *Fantasia in F minor for two pianos*
Mendelssohn: *Songs without words*
Schumann: Piano Concerto in A minor
Chopin: *Preludes, Nocturnes*
Liszt: *Hungarian Rhapsodies*
Brahms: Piano Trio in B major
Mussorgsky: *Pictures at an Exhibition*
Tchaikovsky: Piano Concerto no.1
Grieg: Piano Concerto in A minor
Debussy: *Preludes*
Rachmaninov: Piano Concerto no.2
Ravel: *Concerto for the Left Hand*
Bartók: Piano Concerto no.2
Prokofiev: Piano Concerto no.2
Gershwin: *Rhapsody in Blue*
Shostakovich: Piano Concerto no.1

Many jazz musicians play the piano. You could listen to Scott Joplin, Duke Ellington, Fats Waller, Charles Mingus, Oscar Peterson and Herbie Hancock.

## Index of tunes

# Index